I0782201

Autoimmune Freedom

Transforming Health with Functional Medicine to WIN Your Life Back

Includes free 15 minute consultation!

by

Dr. John Jung

Hardcover ISBN: 978-1-969775-23-9

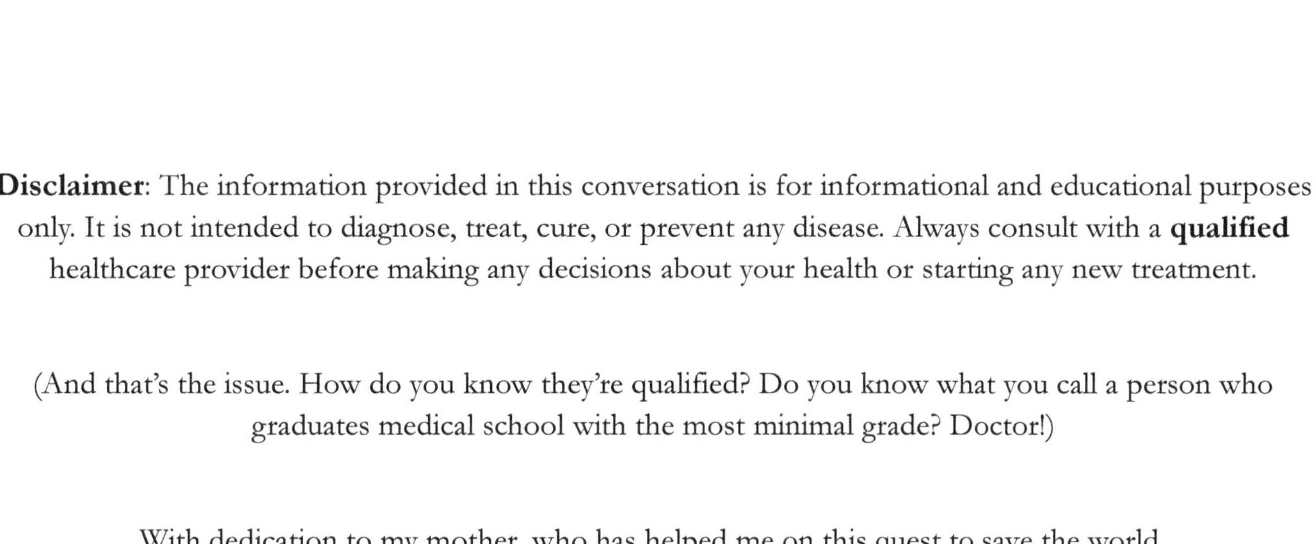

Disclaimer: The information provided in this conversation is for informational and educational purposes only. It is not intended to diagnose, treat, cure, or prevent any disease. Always consult with a **qualified** healthcare provider before making any decisions about your health or starting any new treatment.

(And that's the issue. How do you know they're qualified? Do you know what you call a person who graduates medical school with the most minimal grade? Doctor!)

With dedication to my mother, who has helped me on this quest to save the world.

Hippocrates

There *is* a rapidly growing body of evidence supporting the idea that the way one lives their daily life, and particularly the dietary quality one regularly consumes, *will* influence how long one lives and their quality of life. Hippocrates observed over 2000 years ago, "If we could give every individual the right amount of nourishment and exercise, not too little and not too much, we would have found the safest way to health." Today, research continues to validate Hippocrates' statement, underscoring the value of following a back-to-nature approach to living. Now, we have better ways to test and track that. Why isn't it being done more?

Here are some of my patients with autoimmune issues that responded to functional medicine:

1. Psoriasis and Psoriatic Arthritis: P.J. struggled all her life with psoriasis and psoriatic arthritis despite trying multiple medications. Through functional medicine, we focused on gut healing, tailored nutrition, and addressing root causes. Within months, her symptoms improved significantly, and no medication was necessary.

2. Crohn's Disease: A young woman from San Diego with Crohn's disease, a painful gut inflammatory condition, faced years of minimal relief from conventional treatments. Functional medicine helped her identify and address inflammatory triggers, leading to reduced symptoms, no medications, and knowing what products could lower the inflammatory cytokines.

3. Rheumatoid Arthritis: Joanne suffered from rheumatoid arthritis and turned to functional medicine after: "normal" treatments left her frustrated. By addressing underlying causes and optimizing her health through diet and lifestyle changes, she experienced reduced pain, swelling, and fatigue. Microbiome testing and other analyses were done to see what kept causing flare-ups and mitigate previous damage.

4. Multiple Sclerosis (MS) Patients like Kiara P. have reported reduced symptoms and improved quality of life through personalized interventions. Keeping the myelin healthy, and eliminating her specific epigenetic markers has kept her in remission, as well as most of my clients. Functional medicine protocols for MS often focus on addressing triggers like viral infections, dietary imbalances, and environmental toxins.

5. Hashimoto's Thyroiditis Monica, a 50-year-old female with Hashimoto's, experienced almost 98% relief from fatigue and other symptoms by adopting a phytonutrient-rich diet, eliminating gluten and soy, and incorporating omega-3s, probiotics, NAC, and targeted supplements. Antibodies dropped from the hundreds to 2. And have held these levels for the past 10 years. **We checked** stress and nutrient deficiencies, such as selenium and vitamin D, to reduce thyroid antibodies and thyroglobulin antibodies and improve this immune function, which was attacking the liver and pancreas as well. It is not just a thyroid problem!

6. Adrenal fatigue resolved through functional medicine: Maria A., a stressed-out medical technician, faced extreme fatigue, anxiety, fibrocystic breast, no daytime energy, and excess evening energy, affecting sleep. Functional medicine uncovered gut dysbiosis, low cortisol levels, and leaky gut. After dietary changes, the right testing, and supplements, her problems are minimal. Very grateful to get her life back.

7. Type 2 diabetes (DM2): 1 out of 5 clients see me for this. Often, it's not even related to insulin or obesity; something else is perpetuating the condition. We emphasized nutrient-dense diets, such as low-carb, ketogenic, or Carnivore diets, to improve insulin sensitivity, blood sugar control, and improve gut microbiome balance, which can influence inflammation and glucose metabolism. There is NO reason DM2 cannot be controlled if caught early enough. One of the easier things to "fix".

8 Anxiety: Andrew had years of struggling with anxiety and depression. He felt dismissed and hopeless. By running the proper brain chemicals and stool test for microbiome and leaky gut, he felt better than he can ever remember. He agreed that no doctors actually tried to test the CAUSE of his depression since it's not always psychological; they just kept throwing pills at him, to no avail. There are natural ways to fix it. Only **43.5% of adults** treated with antidepressants in the U.S. achieve remission!

Why this book?

The current medical system is broken. We all know that. Let's empower ourselves today!

The **Americas Health Index (AHI)** is a comprehensive measure that evaluates the overall health and healthcare performance of countries in the Americas region. It considers various factors such as life expectancy, mortality rates, disease prevalence, and healthcare access and quality.

In 2022, the life expectancy in the U.S. was **77.5 years**, while comparable countries averaged **82.2 years.**

Comparison with the Rest of the World

The United States, despite spending significantly more on healthcare per capita compared to other high-income countries, often ranks lower in terms of health outcomes. For example, the U.S. has a lower life expectancy and higher rates of certain health issues like maternal mortality and unmanaged diabetes.

Costs

Healthcare costs in the U.S. are notably higher than in other wealthy nations. In 2022, the U.S. spent an estimated $12,742 per person on healthcare, which is nearly twice as much as the average for other wealthy countries. This high expenditure does not necessarily translate to better health outcomes, highlighting inefficiencies and disparities in the U.S. healthcare system.

Drugs

The United States spends significantly more on prescription drugs compared to other countries. In 2022, the U.S. spent **$1,564 per capita** on pharmaceuticals, which is more than **twice the average** of other wealthy nations, which spent around **$466 per capita.**

While the RDA aims to cover the needs **of almost all healthy individuals**, it is not the absolute minimum required to avoid deficiency diseases. Instead, it provides a buffer to ensure nutritional adequacy for most people, considering varying needs. And then there is the EAR.

The EAR is the average daily nutrient intake level estimated to meet the requirements of **50% of healthy individuals** in a particular life stage and gender group. It's often used to assess the nutrient intakes of groups rather than individuals and can help plan diets for populations.

Number Needed to Treat (NNT) is a measure used in healthcare to determine how many patients need to be treated with a particular therapy or medication to prevent one additional bad outcome (e.g., heart attack, stroke). It's calculated as the inverse of the absolute risk reduction (ARR).

Let's use statins, a common class of cholesterol-lowering medications, as an example:

217 to 250 patients would need to be treated with the statin to prevent ONE additional heart attack or stroke compared to the placebo.

Does this help clarify the concept of NNT for you? Sounds useless to me.

The Number Needed to Treat (NNT) for diabetes prevention can vary depending on the intervention and the population being studied. Here are some examples:

- **Metformin:** For patients at increased risk of developing type 2 diabetes, the NNT for metformin is approximately 7. This means that 7 people need to be treated with metformin for one year to prevent one case of diabetes compared to standard diet and exercise counseling.

- **Lifestyle Modifications:** In the Diabetes Prevention Program (DPP) study, the NNT to prevent one case of diabetes in 3 years through lifestyle modifications (diet and exercise) was 7.

These numbers highlight the effectiveness of lifestyle changes in reducing the risk of developing type 2 diabetes in high-risk individuals.

You are still not in control of your body, or you wouldn't be reading this book.

Obviously, the medical world is lacking in listening to the patient, not considering all causes, and not doing all the needed tests to find out WHY is this happening?

It has been estimated that for every dollar spent on ambulatory medications, another dollar is spent to treat new health problems caused by the medication. When Medicine Hurts Instead of Helps. Washington, DC: The Alliance for Aging Research; 1998.

{Approximately 25% of MDs in the United States are members of the American Medical Association (AMA). For osteopaths (Doctors of Osteopathic Medicine or DOs), about 48% are members of the AMA. In the U.S., it's estimated that around 60-70% of chiropractors belong to a national or regional chiropractic organization, with the American Chiropractic Association (ACA) being the largest. It's disheartening when trust in these organizations is so low.}

Why "Functional Medicine"?

Many functional medicine doctors charge between $3500-50,000 to work with you.

It requires commitment. Motivation. Responsibility. Open communication. And constant questioning of the current data.

Why is it seemingly expensive? I was traveling to present a seminar, and met the head of a local hospital ER at Ohare airport in Chicago. He mentioned his sister got great help from FM, but it "was expensive." I asked him what the average ER cost was, and he had to laugh…

An emergency room visit typically costs from **$150-$3,000** or more, depending on the severity of the condition and what diagnostic tests and treatments are performed. In some cases, especially where critical care is required and/or a procedure or surgery is performed, the cost could reach **$20,000** or more. Have fun deciphering all the hidden charges in the bill and the need for subsequent follow-up with your primary or specialist who does not coordinate care treating the whole person.

And you still aren't fixed.

Medical expenses are a leading cause of bankruptcy in the United States. Each year, around 530,000 American families file for bankruptcy due to medical bills. This accounts for about 62.1% of all bankruptcies in the U.S.

In comparison, medical bankruptcies are much less common in other developed countries with universal healthcare systems, such as France, where they are virtually nonexistent.

"I hate when people can't let go of the past, especially bill collectors." anon.

The reason you're sick and tired is because most doctors are forced into corporate-style medicine. They either don't **listen**, can't or won't **test** for all that's needed, or give the wrong **treatment**. Misdiagnoses can occur for various reasons, and understanding these can help in reducing their occurrence. Here are some common causes:

1. Symptom Overlap: Many medical conditions share similar symptoms, making it challenging to pinpoint the exact cause.

2. Incomplete Patient History: Missing or incomplete information about a patient's medical history can lead to incorrect diagnoses.

3. Communication Barriers: Misunderstandings between patients and healthcare providers, including language barriers, can result in misdiagnoses.

4. Diagnostic Errors: Mistakes in interpreting test results or imaging studies can lead to incorrect conclusions. Usually not all the tests needed are even done.

5. Time Constraints: Healthcare providers often have limited time to spend with each patient, which can lead to rushed assessments and potential errors.

And ending up in the ER (now called ED) wait times here in the Chicago area are from 2.5 hrs. to 5.5 hrs. And their advice when you're done there? Go seek a follow-up doctor. And another and another… and wait and wait… when does it end?

THIS AUTHORS TAKE ON AUTOIMMUNITY in AMERICA:

According to an analysis of US National Center for Health Statistics data. Overall, in 2021, women had an average life expectancy of 79.3 years, and men had an average life expectancy of 73.5 years. The majority of autoimmune diseases are in women. **Well, doesn't that suck?! Live longer with more problems?**

I HAVE LOOKED AT THE MAJORITY of autoimmune information out there, and I am not impressed. Here's what they say: Eliminate eggs, dairy, grains (gluten), food coloring, etc., and the four R's protocol (**Remove, Replace, Re-inoculate, and Repair**) to address the underlying causes of imbalance and aids in alleviating symptoms.

Or they write a story about how they fixed themselves. Great. Boring. We've seen all that.

My readers want FAST answers and not a lot of technical crap to go thru to understand why they feel like their body has betrayed them. Knowing what to fix and then how to fix it.

So, how do you define autoimmune diseases? This means something from the outside affected your systems inside. There are so many ways to detect this through blood, urine, hair, and stool that mainstream medicine is finally trying to utilize, but they are restricted by insurance constraints or the doctor's lack of knowledge.

Epigenetics is the study of changes in organisms caused by modifications in gene expression rather than alterations in the genetic code itself. Essentially, it explores how environmental factors and behaviors—like diet, stress, and exposure to toxins—can influence the way genes are turned "on" or "off" without changing the DNA sequence.

This field has transformed our understanding of genetics, showing that genes are not necessarily set in stone. Epigenetic changes can play a role in development, aging, and even disease susceptibility.

Where is the immune system?

1. Intestinal Immune Tissue (Gut-associated lymphoid tissue, GALT): The gut has a massive presence of immune cells, as it's the largest immune organ in terms of cell numbers.

2. Bone Marrow: This is the primary production site for all immune cells, so it has a high abundance of immature immune cells.

3. Lymph Nodes: These are distributed throughout the body and house many mature immune cells, ready to fight off invaders.

4. Spleen: Contains a significant number of immune cells involved in filtering blood.

5. Thymus: Although smaller, it's where T cells mature, making it crucial for adaptive immunity.

6. Tonsils and Adenoids: These are packed with immune cells but are not as abundant as the other components.

The immune system basically has two parts (called cytokines)

- **B Cells**: These are produced and mature in the bone marrow. Once they are mature, they circulate in the blood and lymphatic system and are essential for producing antibodies, which help to neutralize pathogens.

- **T Cells**: These are also produced in the bone marrow, but they migrate to the thymus, where they mature. T cells play a crucial role in cell-mediated immunity, which involves directly attacking infected cells and coordinating the immune response.

Think of B cells as the body's vigilant antibody producers and T cells as its tactical fighters, each with specialized roles in protecting your body from invaders. Fascinating, right?

So, with the GUT being number one on the list, wouldn't it make sense to start there?!

I like to use cytokine blood test analysis to see what is spiking and what is controlled in your current physiology. These are proteins that determine your disease, and why biologics drugs like Enbrel or Humira were invented.

In the old days, we just threw prednisone steroids to decrease the inflammation but not fix the problem. This book is about the new alternatives with fewer side effects. Your disease is not from a lack of medicine! Please understand that. And taking a biological medicine tips the scale for you to get the new disease. It is ridiculous. Just listen to the ads on TV. "You could die from this stuff, but take it anyway while pictures show people hiking mountains."

Th1 Diseases

Th1 responses are primarily involved in fighting intracellular pathogens like viruses and certain bacteria. They are associated with cell-mediated immunity and involve cytokines such as interferon-gamma (IFN-γ) and tumor necrosis factor (TNF)-β and alpha TNF.

Th2 Diseases (B cells)

Th2 responses are primarily involved in defending against extracellular pathogens like parasites and certain bacteria. They are associated with humoral immunity and involve cytokines such as interleukin-4 (IL-4), IL-5, IL-10, and IL-13. Th2 responses are linked to:

- **Allergic diseases:** such as asthma, allergic rhinitis, and atopic dermatitis.

- **Parasitic infections:** where Th2 responses help in combating parasitic infections.

- **Immunopathological reactions:** including Omenn's syndrome, idiopathic pulmonary fibrosis, and progressive systemic sclerosis.

If your disease isn't listed, you can GOOGLE it, i.e., "cytokines in XYZ disease."

They are regulated by Th17 cells, a subset of T helper cells, and are known for their production of interleukin-17 (IL-17), which plays a significant role in cytokine regulation. IL-17 is involved in promoting inflammation and immune responses.

So, anything that can reduce cytokines, especially TH17, can slow your immune reactions.

If not, a process of NFKB takes over. NF-$\varkappa$B, or nuclear factor kappa B, is a transcription factor that plays a dual role in cell death and survival. It can promote cell survival by inhibiting apoptosis (programmed cell death) through the regulation of anti-apoptotic genes. However, under certain conditions, NF-$\varkappa$B activation can also enhance cell death, particularly in response to stress or damage signals.

NFKB It's about how we resist and eliminate all the external shit, keeping the good stuff to rebuild ourselves. NFKB rules APOPTOSIS, better known as CELL DEATH.

What triggers NFKB? Every negative thing from genetics to insults, to negative people and situations, past surgeries, parasites, DNA damage, drugs preservatives, colorings, radiation etc. How do you slow it? ANTI OXIDANTS and control Inflammation. This is why we all eventually die. It is NOT from a lack of drugs or surgeries. More on this later.

Are we ready for this journey?

Th1 Dominant Diseases:

- Type 1 Diabetes
- Multiple Sclerosis
- Hashimoto's Thyroiditis
- Graves' disease
- Crohn's Disease, Peptic ulcers
- Psoriasis
- Sjögren's Syndrome
- Celiac Disease
- Lichen Planus
- Rheumatoid Arthritis
- Chronic Viral Infections
- Organ-specific autoimmune disorders: including acute kidney allograft rejection and unexplained recurrent abortions.

Th2 Dominant Diseases:

- Lupus
- Allergic Dermatitis
- Scleroderma

- Atopic Eczema

- Sinusitis

- Inflammatory Bowel Disease

- Asthma

- Allergies

- Cancer

- Ulcerative Colitis

- Multiple Chemical Sensitivity

I want you to remember TH17, NFKB, TH1 (TNF Alpha), and TH2 to keep it simple.

Th1 and TH2 have to be treated differently, and the drugs and supplements you take must be meticulously chosen. Do it right, and you don't have the side effects of Biologics, like DEATH. I guess I'm lucky. I haven't killed anyone yet with Functional Medicine.

Common TNF blockers (autoimmune drugs) include:

- **Adalimumab (Humira)**: "Serious infections, including tuberculosis (TB), bacterial sepsis, invasive fungal infections, and other opportunistic infections, have been reported. Some of these infections have been fatal."

- **Infliximab (Remicade)**: "There have been reports of serious infections, including tuberculosis (TB), bacterial sepsis, and invasive fungal infections that may lead to hospitalization or death."

- **Etanercept (Enbrel)**: "Serious infections and malignancies have been reported. These infections may result in hospitalization or death."

- **Rituximab (Rituxan)**: "Severe, including fatal, infusion reactions have been reported. Additionally, severe infections including bacterial, viral, fungal, and new or reactivated viral infections may lead to death."

From web MD: Immunotherapy for Autoimmune Diseases

Conventional autoimmune disease therapy usually involves medications that suppress the body's overall immune system response. As a result, taking immunosuppressant drugs puts you at a higher risk for a variety of infections and illnesses.

Immunotherapy drugs instead target components of the immune system that are causing specific autoimmune conditions such as type 1 diabetes, rheumatoid arthritis (RA), multiple sclerosis (MS), and others. Immunotherapy drugs can help prevent the worsening of symptoms or progression of certain features of an autoimmune disorder.

For example, if you take immunotherapy drugs for MS, those medications won't heal existing lesions in your nervous system, but they may help prevent new lesions from forming.

Does this sound like something you're dying to try!??! The advertisements clearly suggest **death** is a possibility, and yet tens of thousands of people try these dangerous drugs, as if your body forgot what to do to stay healthy???

How do we get started?

First, determine if the problem is inside or outside,

You determine allergies, which will come from an altered immune system, which is mostly from the gut.

- CD4/CD8 ratio blood test,

- Allergy tests, especially Intestinal SigA, IgE

- Stool GI mapping …gut permeability, gut-brain axis, and good vs bad microbes and all that.

- Dutch test, or equivalent to measure hormones made and eliminated, which can also measure nervous system balance, which is the Vagus nerve's sympathetic vs. parasympathetic regulation (fight and flight, vs. relax, digest, and heal)

- Blood cytokines and CRP or ANA with sed rate. Remember when COVID-19 was popular, and you heard about cytokine storms? You are storming all the time with autoimmune reactions!! That's why you feel like crap. Doctors only treat their specialty, not the whole person, even knowing that each system is contingent on the next system. You can't treat a body part, organ, or system in isolation from everything else. That's not homeostasis, and that's not how life works! Everything is linked to everything.

HERE IS THE SIMPLEST EXPLANATION: PEOPLE BREAK AT THEIR WEAKEST LINK. Not the strongest. Is that what doctors' treat? Nope, they chase symptoms. Not causes.

That's why cancer keeps coming back, arthritis gets worse, and you need more and more psychiatric drugs… as if all your problems are from a lack of Prozac, Metamucil, and Opioids?

Find the Cause of the weakest link, and most problems are solved. Every system is codependent on the next system. It's not additive, it's exponential!

You can't treat one aspect of our biological being without expecting a change, positive or negative, in the next.

Why do most patients and doctors forget this?

That's why some people are always healthy, and others are always sick. Their systems have to be balanced from top to bottom.

The weakest link story:

There is a cute story about the parts of the body arguing which was most important.

The eyes declared, "We see everything and spot danger."

The legs said, "We run toward a goal and away from danger".

The hands said, "We were the ones that bring in food and water to the body."

The brain said, "Yeah, but I coordinate all!"

Shortly after, the anus spoke up, stating, "I'm the one that allows the elimination of toxins."

All the others started laughing, so the anus closed up, and after a day, the brain was fatigued, the eyes were blurry, the hands and legs unsteady.

So they did what we always do; they allowed the asshole to be the boss.

The illustration here is obviously that digestion, thinking, and moving are all contingent on elimination and detoxification. Stop putting more crap in your body; let's start removing the bad stuff because it really can't handle anything more.

Autoimmune prefers women

I saw the painful results of this in my family growing up; that's why I became a doctor. According to 2024 data, more than three-quarters of the 24 to 50 million Americans living with autoimmune disease are women, experts say. But I am seeing more and more men with cognitive issues leading them.

According to a Stanford Medicine-led study to be published in the peer-reviewed journal *Cell* in February 2025, some specific autoimmune diseases have particularly notable gender gaps. For example, with lupus, the ratio of female patients to male patients is 9 to 1. For Sjogren's syndrome, it's 19 to 1, Stanford experts note.

What's the difference between men and women? Please, no non-binary definitions.

<u>The Relation Between Testosterone and Immunity?</u>

There is evidence suggesting that lower estrogen levels can have a positive impact on autoimmune conditions in women. Estrogen is known to enhance immune responses, which can sometimes lead to an overactive immune system and contribute to autoimmune diseases. Some key points:

1. Immune Modulation: Studies indicate that estrogen can suppress CD8+ T cells, which are crucial for regulating immune responses. Lower estrogen levels may help restore the balance of these cells, potentially reducing autoimmune activity.

2. Hormonal Influence: Research highlights that autoimmune diseases often fluctuate with hormonal changes, such as during pregnancy or menopause. Lower estrogen levels during menopause, for example, are associated with changes in immune activity.

3. Specific Conditions: Conditions like lupus and rheumatoid arthritis, which are more prevalent in women, have been linked to higher estrogen levels. Reducing estrogen may help mitigate the severity of these diseases.

Stanford Medicine-led study shows why women are at greater risk of autoimmune disease | News Center

There is evidence suggesting that testosterone may help manage autoimmune conditions in both women and men. Testosterone has anti-inflammatory properties and can modulate immune responses, which are often dysregulated in autoimmune diseases.

1. Immune Regulation: Testosterone has been shown to reduce the production of pro-inflammatory cytokines, which are molecules that promote inflammation. This can help mitigate the severity of autoimmune conditions.

2. Gender Differences: Autoimmune diseases are more prevalent in women, who generally have lower levels of testosterone compared to men. This suggests that testosterone may play a protective role.

3. Specific Conditions: Studies have linked low testosterone levels to autoimmune diseases like rheumatoid arthritis and lupus. Testosterone therapy has been explored as a potential treatment to reduce inflammation and improve symptoms.

Some herbs that have been studied for their potential to increase testosterone and decrease estrogen in females, based on medical references, include:

1. Tongkat Ali: Clinical studies have shown that Tongkat Ali supplementation can improve testosterone levels and hormonal balance. It is often used to support physical functioning and libido.

2. Ashwagandha: Known for its adaptogenic properties, Ashwagandha has been studied for its ability to enhance testosterone levels by reducing cortisol, which can negatively impact hormone balance.

3. Tribulus Terrestris: Research suggests that this herb may support testosterone production and help balance estrogen levels.

4. Maca Root: Maca is believed to promote hormonal balance and support testosterone levels, especially in women experiencing hormonal fluctuations.

5. Coleus forskohlii, an Ayurvedic herb, contains forskolin, which has been studied for its potential to increase testosterone levels. Forskolin works by stimulating cyclic adenosine monophosphate (cAMP) production, a messenger that plays a key role in testosterone synthesis. Research suggests that Coleus forskohlii may be particularly effective in overweight and obese individuals, where it has shown improvements in testosterone levels and body composition. Web MD is also good for the heart and eyes.

6. Dehydroepiandrosterone (DHEA) has been studied for its potential impact on autoimmune diseases. Impact of dehydroepiandrosterone on thyroid autoimmunity and function in men with autoimmune hypothyroidism | International Journal of Clinical Pharmacy

1. Thyroid Autoimmunity: A study published in the International Journal of Clinical Pharmacy found that oral DHEA supplementation (50 mg daily) in men with autoimmune hypothyroidism (Hashimoto's thyroiditis) led to a reduction in thyroid peroxidase and thyroglobulin antibodies. This suggests that DHEA may have a beneficial effect on thyroid autoimmunity.

2. Anti-inflammatory Properties: DHEA is known to have anti-inflammatory properties. Some researchers believe that low levels of DHEA could contribute to autoimmune diseases, and supplementation might help restore balance and reduce inflammation.

3. Hormonal Balance: DHEA is a precursor to sex hormones like testosterone and estrogen. Maintaining proper hormonal balance is crucial for immune function, and DHEA supplementation may help in achieving this balance.

Autoimmune diseases often develop quietly, remaining undetected for years before symptoms appear. This highlights the importance of young women regularly checking and monitoring their hormone levels as they age. When DHEA levels fall below the normal range, I collaborate with patients to identify the underlying cause.

A common finding is adrenal fatigue, which triggers a phenomenon called "pregnenolone steal." In this process, the body prioritizes the production of stress hormones over sex hormones. While DHEA supplementation can help restore hormonal balance, it's crucial to uncover the root of this shift using functional medicine principles.

Again, biologics can suppress tumor necrosis factor (TNF) in autoimmune diseases. TNF is a TH1 inhibitor, a type of biological therapy designed to block the activity of TNF, a protein that plays a key role in the inflammation of both TH1 and Th2. By inhibiting TNF, these drugs help reduce inflammation and alleviate symptoms in conditions such as rheumatoid arthritis, psoriatic arthritis, ankylosing spondylitis, and inflammatory bowel disease. It's NFKB, as previously mentioned.

TNF inhibitors work by targeting and neutralizing tumor necrosis factor (TNF), which is a cytokine involved in systemic inflammation. Here's a bit more detail on how they work and their potential side effects:

- **Reducing Symptoms:** By blocking TNF, these medications can help reduce the symptoms of autoimmune diseases, such as joint pain, swelling, and stiffness in rheumatoid arthritis or bowel inflammation in Crohn's disease and ulcerative colitis.

- **Slowing Disease Progression:** In addition to alleviating symptoms, TNF inhibitors can slow the progression of the disease and prevent further joint or tissue damage.

Potential Side Effects:

While TNF inhibitors can be highly effective, they also come with potential side effects, including:

- **Increased Risk of Infections:** Since TNF plays a role in the immune response to infections, blocking it can increase the risk of infections, including serious ones like tuberculosis and fungal infections.

- **Injection Site Reactions:** Common side effects include redness, itching, swelling, or pain at the injection site.

- **Allergic Reactions:** Some patients may experience allergic reactions, ranging from mild to severe.

- **Autoimmune Reactions:** In rare cases, TNF inhibitors can cause the development of new autoimmune conditions, such as lupus-like syndrome or demyelinating disorders.

- **Heart Failure:** TNF inhibitors may exacerbate existing heart failure or lead to new heart failure in some patients.

It is essential for patients to be monitored regularly by their healthcare provider while on TNF inhibitors to manage any potential side effects and ensure the treatment is working effectively.

How about something that doesn't have those harmful effects? Keep reading!

Are you TH-1 or TH-2 dominant? | Dr. K. News

Caffeine, the main active ingredient in coffee, can affect the balance between Th1 and Th2 cells, but its impact can vary depending on individual immune responses. Here's a brief overview:

- **Th1 Dominant:** Individuals with a Th1-dominant immune response might find that caffeine helps reduce their symptoms. Th1 responses are typically associated with conditions like rheumatoid arthritis and multiple sclerosis.

- **Th2 Dominant:** On the other hand, those with a Th2-dominant immune response might experience a worsening of symptoms with caffeine consumption. Th2 responses are often linked to conditions such as asthma and allergies.

To determine if you're Th1 or Th2 dominant, healthcare providers often measure cytokine levels in your blood. Here's a brief overview of the process:

1. Cytokine Testing: Th1 and Th2 cells produce different cytokines, which are signaling proteins that regulate immune responses. Th1 cells produce cytokines like interleukin-2 (IL-2), interleukin-12 (IL-12), tumor necrosis factor alpha (TNF-α), and interferon-gamma (IFN-γ). Th2 cells produce cytokines like interleukin-4 (IL-4), interleukin-13 (IL-13), and interleukin-10 (IL-10).

2. Blood Tests: By measuring the levels of these cytokines in your blood, healthcare providers can determine if you have a Th1 or Th2 dominant immune response.

3. Clinical Symptoms: While cytokine testing is the most accurate method, some general patterns can be observed based on symptoms. Th1 dominance is often associated with organ-specific autoimmune diseases like rheumatoid arthritis and multiple sclerosis, while Th2 dominance is linked to systemic autoimmune diseases and allergies.

I also check the CD4/Cd8 ratios. It tells me if the problem is inside or coming from the outside. The average value is 2.5. Below that points at an internal organ or system not working correctly. Above that, typically, it's any outside invader, toxin, allergy, etc.

Let's discuss wheat (and grains)

Wheat contains a total of 28 allergens that have been identified as causing IgE-mediated allergic reactions. These allergens are in 4 categories;

Wheat contains several allergens that can trigger allergic reactions in some individuals. The primary allergens in wheat are proteins, and there are four main classes of wheat proteins that can cause allergic reactions: 2

1. Albumin

2. Globulin

3. Gliadin

4. Gluten

These proteins can cause symptoms ranging from mild reactions like hives and itching to severe reactions such as anaphylaxis. It's important for individuals with wheat allergies to avoid foods containing these proteins and be aware of hidden sources of wheat in processed foods.

Other allergens: Wheat also contains other allergens like wheat germ agglutinin and various pollen-related allergens, like lectins (neurotoxins).

It's important for individuals with wheat allergies to be aware of these allergens and to avoid foods containing wheat or any of these proteins. And it is sprayed with Round-Up.

Here is some more "research" on gluten:

Healthy Individuals: A study found that consuming gluten did not cause symptoms or fatigue in healthy volunteers. Avoiding gluten does not provide benefits to healthy individuals.

Non-Celiac Gluten Sensitivity (NCGS): A study assessed children with chronic gastrointestinal symptoms but no celiac disease or wheat allergy. Only 39.2% showed a positive response to gluten, indicating NCGS is relatively rare.

Celiac Disease Patients: Yes, allergic

What crap! Stating that 39.2% is a "small percentage" might be misleading, especially given that this figure represents nearly 4 out of 10 children. It's essential to clarify the significance of these results for the broader population.

AVOID: Roundup sprayed grains

Glyphosate, the active ingredient in Roundup, has been shown to suppress cytochrome P450 (CYP) enzymes. Here are some key points from the research:

1. Inhibition of CYP Enzymes: Glyphosate inhibits the activity of CYP enzymes, which play a crucial role in detoxifying xenobiotics (foreign substances) in the body. This inhibition can enhance the damaging effects of other chemical residues and environmental toxins.

2. Impact on Amino Acid Biosynthesis: Glyphosate also disrupts the biosynthesis of aromatic amino acids by gut bacteria. This disruption can lead to various health issues, including gastrointestinal disorders, obesity, diabetes, heart disease, depression, autism, infertility, cancer, and Alzheimer's disease.

3. Synergistic Effects: The suppression of CYP enzymes by glyphosate acts synergistically with other disruptions, such as impaired serum sulfate transport, contributing to the development of modern diseases.

Roundup, which contains the active ingredient **glyphosate**, has been associated with various health concerns, including potential gut issues. Glyphosate can disrupt the gut microbiome by affecting beneficial bacteria, which play a crucial role in maintaining gut health. This disruption can lead to digestive problems, inflammation, and other gut-related issues. WebMd.

Despite its use SEVERAL TIMES during the season, glyphosate is sometimes used to dry grains before harvest. This practice, known as pre-harvest crop desiccation, involves applying glyphosate to crops like wheat, oats, and other grains to accelerate their drying process. This helps farmers harvest the crops more quickly and efficiently, especially in regions with unpredictable weather.

However, this practice has raised concerns about potential glyphosate residues in food products and its impact on human health. If you're looking to minimize your exposure to glyphosate, choosing organic or non-GMO products can be a good option.

A study led by researchers from TGen, part of City of Hope, and Arizona State University shows that pre-clinical models exposed to the herbicide glyphosate develop brain pathologies associated with neurodegenerative disease. The findings suggest the brain may be much more susceptible to the damaging effects of the herbicide than previously thought. Glyphosate, the active ingredient in Roundup, is one of the most pervasive herbicides used in the U.S. and worldwide.

The research, published today in the [Journal of Neuroinflammation](), Dec 2024, identifies an association between glyphosate exposure and symptoms of neuroinflammation, as well as accelerated Alzheimer's disease-like pathology. This study tracks both the presence and impact of glyphosate's byproducts in the brain long after exposure ends, showing an array of persistent, damaging effects on brain health.

Glyphosate and its byproducts can be retained in human tissues. Research has shown that glyphosate can accumulate in various tissues, including the brain. A study found that a byproduct of glyphosate, aminomethylphosphonic acid, can persist in brain tissue even after the exposure ends, raising concerns about its long-term safety for humans. *The National Institutes on Aging, National Cancer Institute of the National Institutes of Health, and ASU Biodesign Institute funded this study.*

There have been concerns and allegations that lobbyists for the agrochemical industry, including those representing glyphosate, have attempted to downplay the potential dangers and cumulative effects of the herbicide. Reports suggest that these lobbyists have influenced regulatory decisions and public perception by funding studies, engaging in public relations campaigns, and lobbying policymakers. What do you think?

And to understand that glyphosate is a complete glycine molecule. It's a perfect match for glycine. Except that it has extra materials stuck onto its nitrogen atom."

Glycine is a very common amino acid your body uses to make proteins, and glyphosate disrupts proteins that depend on glycine.

There is plenty of research that correlates the increase in glyphosate usage (Monsanto's Roundup) to an increase in the incidence of diseases like breast cancer, pancreatic cancer, kidney cancer, thyroid cancer, liver cancer, bladder cancer, and myeloid leukemia.

Glyphosate alters the gut microbiota, reducing beneficial bacteria:

https://www.sciencedirect.com/science/article/abs/pii/S1382668923000911

Many non-GMO grains are sprayed with **Roundup (glyphosate)** as a pre-harvest drying agent. This practice, known as **desiccation**, is used to speed up harvesting and improve yield. Some of the grains commonly treated with glyphosate include:

- Wheat

- Oats

- Barley

- Rye

- Corn (though most corn is genetically modified to be glyphosate-resistant)

- Rice

- Sorghum

Glyphosate is also applied to **legumes** like lentils, chickpeas, and soybeans. If you're looking to avoid glyphosate exposure, choosing **organic grains** or those labeled **glyphosate-free** may be a safer option.

What to do to detox it?

1. Activated Charcoal: Taking activated charcoal after meals can help bind glyphosate and facilitate its excretion.

2. Fermented Foods: Consuming fermented foods like kimchi can help chelate chemicals like glyphosate.

3. Glycine Supplements: Taking glycine supplements can help eliminate glyphosate through urine. (1 gram) twice a day. Or eat lots of meat and gelatine.

4. Organic Produce: Consuming certified organic or home-grown vegetables and fruits can reduce exposure to glyphosate.

5. Bone Broth: Supplementing with organic, grass-fed collagen or making homemade bone broth can boost your intake of glycine, which helps eliminate glyphosate.

Deeper dive into autoimmunity

The lining of the intestine is called the Mucosal Barrier. Your mucosal barrier allows nutrients through, sustaining your health. Many of us have damaged mucosal barriers. The damage can be caused by a number of factors, including stress, infection, toxins, food sensitivity, neurotransmitters, and enzymes.

When the gut becomes "leaky", food particles and bacteria get into the bloodstream that wouldn't normally cross over into the blood. Because the food particles are bigger than the normal metabolites entering the blood, they look like a foreign body to the immune system. When bacteria that normally live in the intestines enter the blood, they are also considered invaders by the immune system. Now, the immune system makes war to attack and kill the invaders. The problem with this is you are now in a state of **chronic systemic inflammation. That can even affect your brain.**

When the gut damage is significant, and more food particles pass the gut wall, you have a "leaky gut". This activates antibodies to form in the bloodstream against one or more of the food particles. Wheat, corn, soy, egg, and dairy are the more common foods people may develop antibodies against. The antibodies bind to many substances, including body tissues that "look similar" to the food. The antibodies then attract "killer cells" to the substances with which they bind, including the body tissues. This damages the tissues and is called an **autoimmune** reaction. The brain is one of the more common areas for this killer cell attack to occur. This causes **neurodegeneration** in the brain. The picture looks like the one below in cases of trauma.

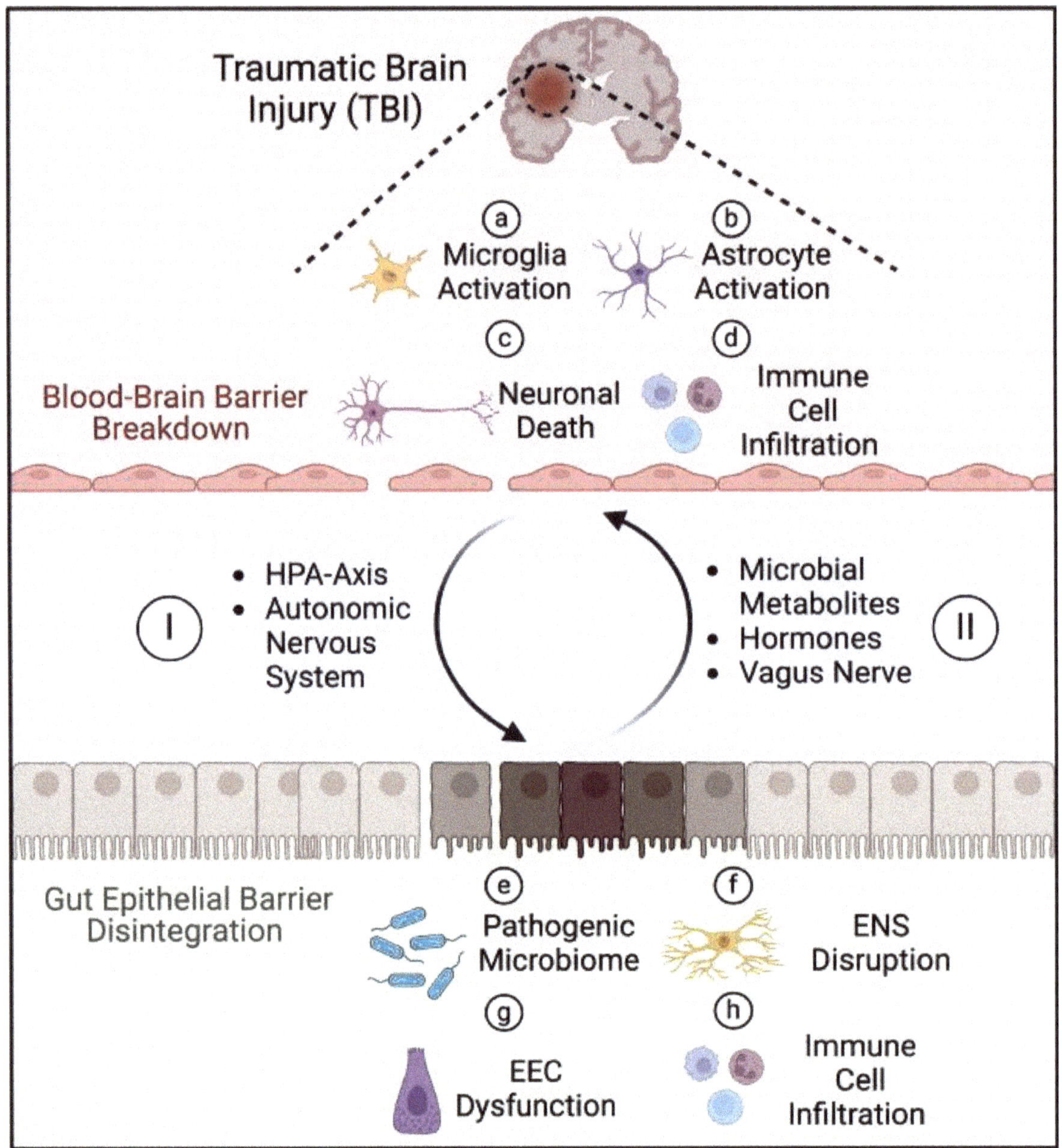

Dysregulated brain-gut axis in the setting of traumatic brain injury: review of mechanisms and anti-inflammatory pharmacotherapies | Journal of Neuroinflammation https://doi.org/10.1186/s12974-024-03118-3

For information on brain trauma and concussions, I have written a book called "ALTERNATIVE TREATMENTS TO TBI: what should you do for brain injury recovery immediately?" See also addendum at end of book (++)

Postural Orthostatic Tachycardia Syndrome (POTS) has been linked to autoimmune conditions, but it is not universally classified as an autoimmune disease. Some research suggests that autoantibodies may play a role in POTS, particularly in cases where it coexists with autoimmune disorders like Sjogren's syndrome, lupus, and celiac disease. Studies have found adrenergic receptor autoantibodies in some POTS patients, indicating a possible autoimmune connection. However, POTS can also develop after viral infections, pregnancy, or physical trauma, making its causes complex and varied.

POTS (Postural Orthostatic Tachycardia Syndrome) is a condition that causes an abnormal increase in heart rate when a person stands up, often accompanied by dizziness, lightheadedness, or fainting. There are several potential causes and contributing factors, including:

1. Autonomic Dysfunction: POTS is often linked to issues with the autonomic nervous system, which controls involuntary functions like heart rate, blood pressure, and digestion. Dysfunction in this system can lead to improper regulation of blood flow and heart rate when standing.

2. Vagus Nerve Dysfunction: Since the vagus nerve plays a major role in regulating heart rate and digestion, problems with this nerve can contribute to POTS symptoms. The vagus nerve helps maintain a balance in the autonomic nervous system, and if it's not functioning properly, it can disrupt normal cardiovascular regulation.

3. Blood Pooling in the Lower Extremities: In some cases, blood can pool in the legs and lower body when standing, leading to insufficient blood flow to the heart and brain, which results in a rapid heart rate (tachycardia) to compensate for the lack of blood circulation.

4. Autoimmune Conditions: POTS can sometimes develop after an infection or illness, particularly in individuals with autoimmune conditions like Ehlers-Danlos syndrome, lupus, or Sjögren's syndrome, where the immune system attacks the body's tissues.

5. Genetic Factors: Some individuals may have a genetic predisposition to developing POTS, particularly those with conditions like hypermobile Ehlers-Danlos syndrome, which affects the connective tissue and can lead to instability in the blood vessels.

6. Trauma or Injury: Physical trauma, especially to the spine or neck, can sometimes trigger or exacerbate POTS symptoms due to its impact on the autonomic nervous system.

7. Chronic Infections or Viral Illnesses: In some cases, a viral infection (like Epstein-Barr virus or COVID-19) can act as a trigger for POTS, leading to prolonged symptoms even after the infection has resolved.

8. Hormonal Changes: Hormonal imbalances, such as those that occur during pregnancy, puberty, or menopause, can sometimes contribute to the development or worsening of POTS symptoms.

You can get a vagal nerve stimulator online for under $100.00 to take care of yourself if standard medicine hasn't helped. And ALWAYS run adrenal testing, other than blood; I prefer saliva, as blood is limited to am and pm cortisol and DHEA. That's not good enough.

POTS Testing for Postural Orthostatic Tachycardia Syndrome (POTS) at home can be a helpful way to gather preliminary data before consulting with a healthcare professional. Here are a couple of common methods:

1. 10-Minute Stand Test

This test involves measuring your heart rate while lying down, sitting, and standing. Here's how you can do it:

Equipment Needed:

- A device to measure heart rate (e.g., Apple Watch, Fitbit, Garmin, or a fingertip pulse oximeter)

- A timer (your smartphone works well)

- A friend to help (optional but helpful)

Procedure:

- Start your heart rate device and set a timer for 15 minutes.

- Lie down completely and relax for 5 minutes.

- At the 5-minute mark, record your heart rate.

- Stand up and continue to record your heart rate every minute for the next 10 minutes.

- Sit down if you feel dizzy or faint.

2. Poor Man's Tilt Table Test

This test is a simplified version of the clinical tilt table test and can be done at home with caution:

Procedure:

- Stand with your heels 6-8 inches from a wall, keeping your shoulders against the wall.

- Measure your heart rate while lying down, sitting, and standing.

- Note any symptoms like dizziness, palpitations, or lightheadedness.

These tests should be done with someone present to assist you. If you feel like you might faint, stop immediately and sit or lie down.

Since the adrenals are affected, you should know what to look for:

Ragland's Test is a simple, non-invasive test used to assess adrenal function by measuring blood pressure changes. Here's how it works: Ragland's Test is used to diagnose orthostatic hypotension. Orthostatic hypotension is defined as a significant drop in blood pressure when standing up from a sitting or lying position. During Ragland's Test, blood pressure and heart rate are measured after lying down for a few minutes and then again after standing up for one to three minutes. A drop in systolic blood pressure of 20 mm Hg or more, or a drop in diastolic blood pressure of 10 mm Hg or more, indicates orthostatic hypotension.

1. Lie Down: Have your blood pressure measured while lying down for a few minutes.

2. Stand U: Immediately stand up and measure your blood pressure again after 1 minute.

3. Compare In a healthy individual, the systolic blood pressure should rise by 8-10 mmHg. If the systolic pressure doesn't rise or drop, it may indicate adrenal insufficiency.

Eye Pupil Reaction Test for Adrenal Function

The eye pupil reaction test, also known as the pupillary light reflex test, can provide insights into adrenal function. Here's how it's typically conducted:

1. Prepare: Sit in a dimly lit room to allow your pupils to dilate naturally.

2. Flashlight: Use a flashlight or penlight to shine a light into one eye for about 15-20 seconds.

3. Observe: Watch the reaction of the pupil in the illuminated eye. Normally, the pupil should constrict (get smaller) when exposed to light.

Interpretation:

- **Normal Response:** The pupil constricts quickly and remains constricted while the light is shining.

- **Adrenal Insufficiency:** If the pupil initially constricts but then begins to pulsate or dilate despite the light being present, it may indicate adrenal insufficiency. This reaction is sometimes referred to as the "pupil fatigue" response.

- **Hypoadrenia:** In cases of adrenal fatigue, the pupil may also show a slower response to light or remain dilated longer after the light is removed.

This is why we obtain saliva cortisol levels 4 times a day. It's in a kit called DUTCH TEST.

If adrenal cortisol is high:

You can adopt lifestyle changes and incorporate certain foods and supplements.

Lifestyle Changes

1. Prioritize Sleep: Aim for 7–9 hours of quality sleep per night. Establish a consistent sleep schedule and create a calming bedtime routine.

2. Exercise Regularly: Moderate-intensity activities like walking, yoga, or swimming can help reduce stress.

3. Limit Caffeine: High caffeine intake can elevate cortisol, so consider reducing consumption.

Supplement with:

1. Omega-3 Fatty Acids: Found in fish like salmon, walnuts, and flaxseeds, omega-3s can help regulate cortisol.

2. Vitamin D: Sunlight exposure or supplements can support hormonal balance.

3. Dark Chocolate: Rich in antioxidants, it may help lower cortisol levels.

4. Adaptogenic Herbs: Ashwagandha and Rhodiola are known for their stress-reducing properties. Consult a healthcare provider for appropriate doses.

5. Magnesium: Found in leafy greens, nuts, and seeds, magnesium can help manage stress.

For low cortisol levels, certain adaptogenic herbs can help:

Licorice Root (Glycyrrhiza glabra): Helps prolong the action of cortisol in the body. Dosage: 200–400 mg of standardized extract daily. Avoid prolonged use without medical supervision.

1. Ashwagandha (Withania somnifera): Balances cortisol levels and supports adrenal health. Dosage: 300–600 mg of standardized extract daily.

2. Rhodiola Rosea: Enhances energy and reduces fatigue. Dosage: 200–400 mg of standardized extract daily.

3. Panax Ginseng (Asian Ginseng): Stimulates adrenal function and boosts energy. Dosage: 200–400 mg of standardized extract daily.

4. Eleuthero (Siberian Ginseng): Supports physical and mental stamina. Dosage: 300–600 mg of standardized extract daily.

Managing Postural Orthostatic Tachycardia Syndrome **(POTS)** often involves a combination of lifestyle modifications and medical treatments.

Lifestyle Adjustments

- **Increase Fluid & Salt Intake**: Drinking **2-3 liters** of water daily and consuming **3-10 grams** of salt can help maintain blood volume and circulation.

- **Compression Garments**: Wearing **compression socks or abdominal binders** (20-30 mmHg pressure) can improve blood flow.

- **Exercise**: **Recumbent or resistance training** can help strengthen circulation, but pacing is crucial to avoid worsening symptoms.

- **Avoid Prolonged Standing**: Sitting when possible and using stools for activities like brushing teeth can conserve energy.

- **Temperature Regulation**: Avoiding **high heat and humidity** can prevent symptom flare-ups.

- **Elevate Head of Bed**: Raising the head of the bed by **4-12 inches** can help with fluid retention overnight.

For **POTS (Postural Orthostatic Tachycardia Syndrome)**, the best type of salt is one that provides **adequate sodium** without unnecessary additives. Here are some commonly recommended options:

- **Sea Salt**: Contains trace minerals that may support electrolyte balance.

- **Himalayan Pink Salt**: Naturally rich in minerals like potassium and magnesium.

- **Real Salt (from Utah)**: A natural, unprocessed salt with beneficial minerals.

- **Salt Tablets**: Convenient for controlled sodium intake, often used by POTS patients.

- **Electrolyte Salt Mixes**: Some brands combine sodium with potassium and magnesium for better hydration.

- **Celtic salt** is a mineral-rich sea salt that contains **magnesium, potassium, calcium, and iron**. Some POTS patients prefer it because of its **natural mineral content**, which may support electrolyte balance. Like Himalayan salt, it has a **moist texture and grayish hue**, distinguishing it from refined table salt.

- If you're considering Celtic salt for POTS, it can be used similarly to other salts—**adding it to water or meals** to help maintain sodium levels. Some practitioners recommend **about 1 teaspoon per day** in water for electrolyte support.

Some POTS patients prefer **non-iodized salt** to avoid excess iodine intake, while others find **salt sticks** helpful for maintaining sodium levels throughout the day. It's important if you have thyroid issues.

HINT: If you <u>can't go to sleep</u>, your adrenals are <u>overfiring</u> cortisol. If you <u>can't stay asleep,</u> your adrenals are fatigued, and your body wakes you up to get an energy source. That's why we test them to see if they are high are low. Symptoms can be the same!

The two Viruses you should always check>>>CMV and EBV, H. Pylori (bacteria)

CMV has been linked to increased severity of COVID-19 and other infections, but again, this is due to its natural properties and not any form of genetic engineering. Cytomegalovirus (CMV) was first proposed as a term by Weller and colleagues in 1960 to replace older names like "cytomegalic inclusion disease" and "salivary gland virus". CMV infections in children can sometimes lead to gastrointestinal issues, including stomach problems.

As for treatment, while there are antiviral medications available for CMV infections, such as ganciclovir and valganciclovir, these treatments are not always effective for everyone. Additionally, CMV can remain latent in the body and reactivate, making it challenging to completely eliminate. There are newer antiviral medications like Letermovir and Maribavir that have shown promise, but they are not without limitations and side effects.

Tagamet, also known by its generic name **cimetidine**, is an over-the-counter medication primarily used to treat heartburn and stomach ulcers by reducing stomach acid. Interestingly, there is some evidence suggesting that cimetidine may have antiviral properties and could be helpful in treating Cytomegalovirus (CMV and other herpes viruses. Once a day for 60 days

Studies have shown that cimetidine can shorten the duration of herpes outbreaks and prevent recurrences by modulating immune function. Also decreases stomach acid, so caution.

Discovery of EBV

In 1964, Michael Anthony Epstein and Yvonne Barr, while working at the University of London, discovered and isolated the Epstein-Barr Virus from the cells of a patient with Burkitt lymphoma. This discovery marked the first time a virus was linked to a specific type of human cancer.

- **Infectious Mononucleosis:** EBV is the primary cause of infectious mononucleosis, also known as "mono" or the "kissing disease," which is characterized by fever, sore throat, and swollen lymph nodes.

- **Cancer Associations:** EBV has been linked to several types of cancers, including Burkitt lymphoma, Hodgkin lymphoma, and nasopharyngeal carcinoma.

- **Autoimmune Diseases:** Research suggests that EBV may play a role in the development of certain autoimmune diseases, such as multiple sclerosis and systemic lupus erythematosus.

- **Chronic Infections:** EBV can lead to chronic infections in some individuals, particularly those with compromised immune systems.

- **Cytomegalovirus (CMV)** is particularly dangerous for individuals with AIDS (Acquired Immunodeficiency Syndrome). CMV can cause severe complications in AIDS patients, especially those with advanced immunosuppression. Before the advent of effective antiretroviral therapy (ART), CMV infections were a common and serious opportunistic infection in AIDS patients, leading to conditions like CMV retinitis, esophagitis, and colitis.

While Epstein - Barr virus (EBV) can also affect individuals with weakened immune systems, including those with AIDS, CMV is more commonly associated with severe and life-threatening complications in this population. Many of us have chronic EBV, especially **long COVID** patients.

The Epstein-Barr virus (EBV) is associated with several other diseases beyond infectious mononucleosis (mono).

1. Autoimmune Diseases: EBV is associated with an increased risk of autoimmune diseases such as systemic lupus erythematosus (SLE), rheumatoid arthritis (RA), multiple sclerosis (MS), and juvenile idiopathic arthritis (JIA).

2. Inflammatory Bowel Disease (IBD): EBV has been linked to conditions like Crohn's disease and ulcerative colitis.

3. Celiac Disease: There is evidence suggesting a connection between EBV and celiac disease.

4. Type 1 Diabetes: EBV is also associated with an increased risk of developing type 1 diabetes.

5. Certain Cancers: EBV is linked to various cancers, including Burkitt lymphoma, Hodgkin's lymphoma, and nasopharyngeal carcinoma.

6. Chronic fatigue Syndrome, Hashimoto thyroid.

(Many of us have chronic EBV, especially long covid patients) and CMV

Herbs with Antiviral & Immune-Supporting Properties

There are several natural herbs, amino acids, and nutrients that may help support the immune system and manage chronic Epstein - Barr virus (EBV).

Dosage guidelines for the herbs, amino acids, and nutrients commonly used to support **chronic Epstein - Barr virus (EBV)**:

Herbs with Antiviral & Immune-Supporting Properties

- **Lemon Balm**: **300-1200 mg** per day or **40-60 drops** of tincture. #1 for me.
- **Olive Leaf Extract**: **500-1000 mg** per day.
- **Elderberry**: **300-600 mg** per day or **1 teaspoon of syrup 2-4 times daily**.
- **Astragalus**: **500-1000 mg** per day.
- **Cat's Claw**: **500-1000 mg** per day.
- **Licorice Root**: **400-800 mg** per day (use cautiously if you have high blood pressure).
- **Reishi Mushroom**: **1000-3000 mg** per day.

Amino Acids & Nutrients

- **L-Lysine: 1000-3000 mg** per day.
- **Glutathione: 250-500 mg** per day.
- **N-Acetyl Cysteine (NAC): 600-1200 mg** per day.

- **Zinc: 30-50 mg** per day.

- **Vitamin C: 1000-3000 mg** per day.

- **Vitamin D: 2000-5000 IU** per day.

- **Selenium: 100-200 mcg** per day.

Monolaurin is often used for immune support and antiviral properties, especially for Epstein - Barr virus **(EBV)**.

- **Starting Dose**: **300-600 mg** per day to assess tolerance.

- **Moderate Dose**: **1200-2400 mg** per day for ongoing immune support.

- **Higher Dose**: Some protocols suggest **up to 6000 mg** per day, divided into multiple doses.

Bovine colostrum is often used for immune support and viral defense, but dosages can vary based on individual needs. Here are general recommendations:

- **General Immune Support: 3-6 grams** per day.

- **Gut Health & Leaky Gut Repair: 10-20 grams** per day.

- **Athletic Performance & Recovery: Up to 20 grams** per day.

Taking pancreatic digestive enzymes may prolong a GOOD life. I believe in them since digesting food can poorly impact hormone balance and potentially contribute to telomere damage, especially if the digestive process is inefficient or if the diet is poor.

1. Hormone Burnout: Chronic stress and poor digestion can lead to an imbalance in hormones, particularly cortisol, which is known as the "stress hormone." When the body is constantly in a state of stress, digestion becomes less efficient, and this can contribute to hormonal imbalances and burnout.

2. Telomere Damage: Poor diet and chronic stress can also accelerate telomere shortening, which is associated with aging and various chronic diseases. A healthy diet rich in antioxidants, whole grains, and nutrients can help protect telomeres and slow down their shortening.

Probiotics help maintain a healthy balance of gut bacteria, which can improve digestion, boost the immune system, and even positively impact mental health. Digestive enzyme supplements aid in breaking down food, ensuring better nutrient absorption and reducing digestive discomfort.

Diet Influences Telomere Shortening: Eating Your Way to the Fountain of Youth?

Fiber and polyphenols are essential for maintaining a healthy gut microbiome. Here's how they work:

Fiber

- **Prebiotic Effect**: Fiber serves as food for beneficial gut bacteria, promoting their growth and activity.

- **Short-Chain Fatty Acids (SCFAs)**: When gut bacteria ferment fiber, they produce SCFAs like butyrate, which support gut lining health and reduce inflammation.

- **Sources**: Whole grains, fruits (like apples and bananas), and vegetables (like broccoli and carrots).

Metamucil is a good fiber source. Its main ingredient is **psyllium husk,** a type of soluble fiber that offers several health benefits:

- **Digestive Health**: Helps relieve constipation and improve bowel regularity.

- **Heart Health**: Can lower cholesterol levels when combined with a healthy diet.

- **Blood Sugar Control**: This may help stabilize blood sugar levels in people with diabetes.

Polyphenols

- **Antioxidant Properties**: Polyphenols help reduce oxidative stress and inflammation in the gut.

- **Microbial Modulation**: They suppress harmful bacteria while encouraging the growth of beneficial ones.

- **Sources**: Berries, green tea, dark chocolate, red wine (in moderation), and spices like turmeric.

The combination of fiber and polyphenols creates a **synergistic effect**, enhancing gut health by improving microbial diversity and reducing inflammation.

Short-chain fatty acids (SCFAs) play a crucial role in maintaining gut health. They are produced when beneficial gut bacteria ferment dietary fiber: The three main SCFAs are acetate, propionate, and butyrate: Dietary Fiber and Gut Health (https://www.verywellhealth.com/short-chain-fatty-acids-5219806). Here's how they contribute to gut health:

1. Energy Source: SCFAs, especially butyrate, provide energy to the cells lining the colon.

2. Reducing Inflammation: SCFAs help reduce inflammation in the gut, which is important for preventing conditions like inflammatory bowel disease (IBD).

3. Maintaining Gut Barrier: SCFAs strengthen the gut barrier, preventing harmful substances from entering the bloodstream.

4. Regulating Immune System: SCFAs play a role in regulating the immune system, helping to maintain a balanced immune response.

5. Promoting Healthy Gut Flora\: SCFAs support the growth of beneficial gut bacteria, which in turn produce more SCFAs.

Incorporating fiber-rich foods like chia seeds and flaxseeds into your diet can help promote the production of SCFAs and support overall gut health.

Both butter and apple cider vinegar can contribute to the production of short-chain fatty acids (SCFAs) in the gut, but in different ways:

1. Butter contains butyrate, one of the main SCFAs. Butyrate is produced by beneficial gut bacteria when they ferment dietary fiber. Consuming butter can provide a direct source of butyrate, which helps maintain the gut lining, reduce inflammation, and support overall gut health. Butyrate is produced by several types of beneficial gut bacteria, primarily Firmicutes and Actinobacteria. These bacteria ferment dietary fibers, producing butyrate as a byproduct. Some specific genera of bacteria known to produce butyrate include Faecalibacterium, Clostridium, and Eubacterium.

2. Apple cider vinegar is a fermented liquid that contains acetate, another type of SCFA. Acetate is produced by gut bacteria during the fermentation process and helps nourish butyrate-producing microbes in the gut. Consuming apple cider vinegar can support the production of SCFAs and promote a healthy gut environment.

To increase propionate in your diet, focus on consuming foods rich in beta-glucans, a type of soluble fiber that promotes the production of propionate by gut bacteria. Here are some great options:

1. Chicory Roo: This root is high in inulin, a type of prebiotic fiber that can promote the production of propionate.

2. Garlic and Onions: These vegetables contain prebiotic fibers that support gut bacteria and propionate production.

3. Akkermansia muciniphila lays a significant role in maintaining gut health. Here are some key functions: It is available online.

4. Maintaining Gut Barrier: Akkermansia helps strengthen the gut lining by degrading mucin (a component of the mucus layer) and producing short-chain fatty acids (SCFAs) like acetate and propionate. This supports the integrity of the gut barrier and prevents "leaky gut".

5. Regulating Immune Response: By maintaining the gut barrier, Akkermansia helps regulate the immune system and reduces inflammation.

6. Metabolic Health: Studies suggest that Akkermansia is associated with improved metabolic health, including better glycemic control, lower serum lipid levels, and reduced risk of obesity and type 2 diabetes.

7. Protecting Against Diseases: Akkermansia has been linked to lower rates of cardiovascular disease, inflammatory bowel disease, and other chronic conditions.

Including prebiotics like dietary fibers and polyphenols in your diet can help support the growth of Akkermansia and promote overall gut health. Or you can just buy the pill online.

All these foods in your diet can help promote a healthy gut microbiome and increase the production of propionate, which has various health benefits, including regulating appetite and controlling blood glucose levels. SCFA: mechanisms and functional importance in the gut | Proceedings of the Nutrition Society | Cambridge Core

Benefits of **probiotics during pregnancy in** reducing disease in infants:

1. Probiotics Decrease Morbidity and Mortality in Preemies - This study published in AAP Grand Rounds found that probiotics reduced all-cause mortality and severe Necrotizing enterocolitis (NEC) in preterm infants. The study involved a meta-analysis of randomized trials and showed that combinations of Lactobacillus spp and Bifidobacterium spp were particularly effective.

2. Probiotics in Pregnancy: A Study on Maternal and Infant Health - This study aimed to assess if supplementation with **Lactobacillus rhamnosus HN001** during pregnancy and breastfeeding could reduce rates of infant eczema, atopic sensitization, and maternal gestational diabetes mellitus.

3. Use of Probiotics in Preterm Infants- Published in Pediatrics, this clinical report reviewed the efficacy of probiotics in reducing Necrotizing enterocolitis and all-cause mortality in preterm infants. The report highlighted that multiple-strain probiotics showed significant benefits. (PDF) The Probiotics in

Pregnancy Study (PiP Study): rationale and design of a double-blind, randomized controlled trial to improve maternal health during pregnancy and prevent infant eczema and allergy

AND <u>never supplement</u> with folic acid, a key ingredient in prenatal supplements. MOST obstetricians forget this…

If you have the MTHFR gene activated, and most of us do, it will cause more harm than benefit. Its job is to detoxify the developing body and avoid neural tube defects.

So take **5 METHYL FOLATE**… which is the safe form. Also great for a mother's depression!!!

BEANS in the diet?

"Eat right for your blood type"? Or Gundry diet???

One of the central theories of these diets has to do with proteins called <u>lectins</u>. These are a family of proteins that can bind to carbohydrate molecules.

Overall, it appears that the majority of agglutinating lectins react with all ABO blood types. Lectins are known as NUEROTOXINS. So, I'll agree to minimize beans.

Red kidney beans are toxic if they are not cooked properly. They contain a lectin, specifically phytohemagglutinin (PHA), which can cause food poisoning if consumed in high amounts. Symptoms of poisoning include nausea, vomiting, and diarrhea. To avoid this, it's important to soak red beans for at least 5 hours, discard the soaking water, and then boil them in fresh water for at least 30 minutes. Slow cookers should be avoided, as they don't reach a high enough temperature to destroy the toxins.

White beans, also known as cannellini beans or navy beans, are packed with nutritional benefits. Here are some highlights:

1. Rich in Fiber: White beans are an excellent source of dietary fiber, <u>which helps slow down the absorption of carbohydrates</u>. This can help regulate blood sugar levels and keep you feeling fuller for longer.

2. High in Protein: They are a great plant-based protein source, making them a good option for vegetarians and vegans.

3. Packed with Nutrients: White beans provide essential vitamins and minerals, including iron, magnesium, and folate, which are important for overall health.

4. Low in Fat: They are naturally low in fat, making them a healthy addition to your diet.

Garbanzo beans (also known as chickpeas) and hummus (a spread made from chickpeas, tahini, olive oil, and lemon juice) can be great additions to diets aimed at bodybuilding, managing autoimmune conditions and controlling diabetes, although they still have lectins.

1. Bodybuilding

Garbanzo beans are a good source of plant-based protein, which is essential for muscle repair and growth. They also provide fiber and complex carbohydrates, which can help sustain energy levels during workouts. Incorporating garbanzo beans into meals like salads, soups, and stews can support muscle-building efforts.

2. Autoimmune Diets

Hummus contains ingredients like chickpeas, tahini, and olive oil, which have anti-inflammatory properties. Olive oil, in particular, is rich in antioxidants that can help reduce inflammation. Including hummus in your diet can be beneficial for managing autoimmune conditions by promoting overall gut health and reducing inflammation.

3. Diabetic Diets

Hummus has a low glycemic index, meaning it causes a slow and steady rise in blood sugar levels. This makes it a suitable snack for people with diabetes. The fiber and protein in hummus can help regulate blood sugar levels and keep you feeling full, which is important for managing diabetes.

Carnivore diet is what I mostly recommend for its potential effects on autoimmune diseases:

1. A meat-only diet is not the answer, says Mato: "Examining the carnivore and Lion Diets." - This article from Mayo Clinic Press examines the carnivore diet and its potential impact on health. It highlights that while some individuals report improvements in autoimmune symptoms, there is limited scientific evidence to support the long-term safety and efficacy of the diet. (So they stopped doing a longer study)

2. The Harvard Carnivore Diet Study: Findings and Takeaway - This study conducted by Harvard University surveyed over 2,000 individuals following the carnivore diet and found mixed results. While some participants reported health improvements, the study emphasized the need for further research to understand the diet's long-term effects.

When a study says it needs further research, it means we are on the right track to keep researching.

2021 Carnivore Diet

<u>The Harvard Carnivore Diet Study: Findings and Takeaway - Dr. Robert Kiltz</u>

The **Specific Carbohydrate Diet (SCD)** is a restrictive, grain-free diet designed to help manage gastrointestinal conditions like Crohn's disease:

Here's a general outline of what foods are included and excluded from the SCD:

Allowed Foods

- **Meats:** Without additives, poultry, fish, shellfish, and eggs.

- **Certain Legumes:** Dried navy beans, lentils, peas, split peas, unroasted cashews, peanuts in a shell, all-natural peanut butter, and lima beans.

- **Dairy:** Limited to cheeses such as cheddar, Colby, Swiss, dry curd cottage cheese, and homemade yogurt fermented for at least 24 hours.

- **Vegetables:** Most fresh, frozen, raw, or cooked vegetables and string beans.

- **Fruits:** Fresh, raw, cooked, frozen, or dried fruits with no added sugar.

- **Nuts and Nut Flours:** Most nuts and nut flours.

- **Oils:** Most oils, teas, coffee, mustard, cider, white vinegar, and juices with no additives or sugars.

- **Sweeteners:** Honey as a sweetener.

Prohibited Foods

- **Sugars:** Sugar, molasses, maple syrup, sucrose, processed fructose, including high-fructose corn syrup, and any processed sugar.

- **Grains:** All grains, including corn, wheat, wheat germ, barley, oats, rice, and others. This includes bread, pasta, and baked goods made with grain-based flour.

- **Canned Vegetables:** Canned vegetables with added ingredients.

- **Starchy Tubers:** Starchy tubers such as potatoes, sweet potatoes, and turnips.

- **Processed Meats:** Canned and most processed meats.

- **Milk Products High in Lactose:** Milk and milk products high in lactose such as mild cheddar, commercial yogurt, cream, sour cream, and ice cream.

- **Candy and Chocolate:** Candy, chocolate, and products that contain FOS (fructooligosaccharides).

The SCD works by eliminating complex carbohydrates that are hard to digest, which can lead to bacterial overgrowth and irritation in the intestines: Reviewing How It Works - WebMD](https://www.webmd.com/ibd-crohns-disease/crohns-disease/specific-carbohydrate-diet-overview). By consuming only easily digestible carbohydrates, the diet aims to prevent this overgrowth and reduce inflammation.

I believe it's better to avoid any carbohydrate other than a mix of berries, with their huge content of polyphenols. Polyphenols are powerful antioxidants found in many plant-based foods.

- **Cloves** – The highest known source, with **15,188 mg per 100g.**

- **Dried Peppermint – 11,960 mg per 100g.**

- **Star Anise – 5,460 mg per 100g.**

- **Cocoa Powder – 3,448 mg per 100g.**

- **Dark Chocolate – 1,664 mg per 100g.**

- **Black Elderberries – 1,359 mg per 100g.**

- **Blueberries – 560 mg per 100g.**

- **Blackcurrants – 758 mg per 100g.**

- **Hazelnuts – 495 mg per 100g.**

- **Pecans – 493 mg per 100g.**

These foods are excellent sources of polyphenols, which may support **heart health, brain function, and inflammation reduction**.

Coconut yogurt can be a **beneficial option** for individuals managing autoimmune conditions, especially those following the **Autoimmune Protocol (AIP)** or avoiding dairy. It is **dairy-free**, which can be helpful for those with sensitivities to cow's milk, and it contains **probiotics** that support gut health—a key factor in autoimmune wellness.

However, the benefits depend on the **ingredients**. Some store-bought coconut yogurts contain **added sugars, gums, and preservatives**, which may not be ideal for inflammation management. Choosing **unsweetened, probiotic-rich coconut yogurt** or making your own can be a better option.

Coconut yogurt brands that may be good lactose-free options for autoimmune-friendly diets:

- **Siggi's Plain Plant-Based Coconut Yogurt** – High in protein and low in sugar, making it a great choice for smoothies and snacks.

- **So Delicious Dairy Free Coconut Milk Yogurt** – Vegan, gluten-free, and made with organic coconut milk.

- **Harmless Harvest Organic Plain Coconut Yogurt** – Known for its clean ingredients and rich, creamy texture.

- **Cocojune Organic Pure Coconut Yogurt** – A smooth, mild-flavored option that works well in dips and recipes.

I recommend a daily smoothie with berries or use this as your breakfast.

Fungus loves carbohydrates. Hence, please limit fruits (pure carbohydrates) to berries.

Fungal influences on autoimmune diseases are an emerging area of research. Here are some key findings from recent studies:

1. Fungal Pathogens and Immune Recognition Fungal pathogens are recognized by the immune system through pattern recognition receptors (PRRs) on cells like dendritic cells and macrophages. This recognition can lead to the development of Th1 and Th17 immune responses, which are involved in autoimmune diseases.

2. Gut Health and Autoimmunity: The gut microbiome, including fungi, plays a crucial role in immune system regulation. Dysbiosis, or an imbalance in gut microbiota, can contribute to autoimmune conditions like rheumatoid arthritis and ulcerative colitis.

3. Potential Therapeutic Approaches: Controlling fungal populations in the gut microbiota could improve gut health and reduce the risk of autoimmune diseases. Probiotics and other interventions targeting gut microbiota are being explored as potential treatments. Immune responses to fungal pathogens | British Society for Immunology

The relationship between **fungi and cancer** is ongoing.

1. Mycobiome and Cancer: Recent studies have shown that various fungal species, collectively known as the mycobiome, can be found within cancerous tumors. These fungi may interact with bacteria, cellular proteins, and immune cells, potentially influencing cancer progression and patient prognosis.

2. Fungal Presence in Tumors: Research has identified fungi in tumors arising from at least 35 different tissues. The presence of fungi like Candida has been associated with inflammation, immune activation, and tumor-promoting gene expression changes in cancers such as stomach, head-and-neck, and colon cancers.

<u>**The Fungus Within Us:**</u> <u>The Mycobiome's Emerging Role in Cancer - American Association for Cancer Research (AACR)</u>

An antifungal diet aims to reduce fungal overgrowth in the body by avoiding foods that promote yeast and fungi and including foods with antifungal properties. Here are some key components of an antifungal diet:

Foods to Eat

- **Garlic:** Contains alicin, a potent antifungal compound.
- **Coconut Oil:** Rich in caprylic acid, which can kill yeasts.
- **Ginger:** Contains gingerols and shogaols, which have antifungal properties.
- **Onions:** High in sulfur compounds that may help fight fungi.
- **Pumpkin Seeds:** The fats in pumpkin seeds can help eliminate yeasts and fungi.
- **Lemon and Lime:** High in vitamin C, which can assist in killing yeasts and fungi.
- **Non-Starchy Vegetables:** Such as leafy greens, broccoli, and cauliflower.
- **Lean Proteins:** Chicken, turkey, and fish.

Foods to Avoid

- **Sugar:** Yeasts and fungi thrive on sugar.
- **Refined Carbohydrates:** Such as white bread, pasta, and pastries.
- **Alcohol:** Can promote yeast overgrowth.
- **Most Dairy Products:** Especially those high in lactose. Use Kefir.
- **Processed Foods:** Often contain hidden sugars and unhealthy fats.
- **Most Fruits and juices:** High in sugar, such as bananas, grapes, and mangoes.

Sample Meal Plan

- **Breakfast:** Scrambled eggs with spinach and garlic, served with a side of sautéed mushrooms.
- **Lunch:** Grilled chicken salad with mixed greens, avocado, and a lemon-garlic dressing.
- **Dinner:** Baked salmon with a side of steamed broccoli and a coconut oil drizzle.
- **Snacks:** Sliced carrots with hummus, a handful of pumpkin seeds, or a small serving of plain Greek yogurt.

Natural antifungal herbs:

1. Garlic

- **Active Compound:** Allicin
- **Dosage:** 2-4 fresh cloves daily or 600-1200 mg of garlic extract.
- **Use:** Effective against Candida and other fungal infections.

2. Oregano Oil

- **Active Compound:** Carvacrol
- **Dosage:** 100-200 mg of oregano oil capsules or 2-3 drops diluted in water daily.
- **Use:** Potent antifungal properties, especially for gut health. Only for 2 weeks!

3. Pau d'Arco

- **Active Compound:** Lapachol
- **Dosage:** 1-2 cups of tea daily or 500-1000 mg in capsule form.
- **Use:** Helps combat yeast infections and skin fungi.

4. Turmeric

- **Active Compound:** Curcumin
- **Dosage:** 500-2000 mg of curcumin extract daily.
- **Use:** Reduces fungal growth and inflammation.

5. Coconut Oil

- **Active Compound**: Caprylic Acid
- **Dosage**: 1-3 tablespoons daily.
- **Use**: Effective against Candida and other fungi.

Adendum:

The Scientific role of NF-$\varkappa$B in Perpetuating Autoimmune diseases:

https://youtu.be/OnI-14unJaA

NF-$\varkappa$B (nuclear factor kappa-light-chain-enhancer of activated B cells) (as it is also responsible for TH1 cells as well.)

It is a protein complex that regulates the expression of genes involved in immune responses, inflammation, and cell survival. Dysregulation of NF-$\varkappa$B signaling is implicated in various autoimmune diseases due to its role in promoting inflammation and immune responses.

1. Regulation of Immune Responses: NF-κB regulates genes involved in immune responses, inflammation, and cell survival. It is activated by various stimuli, including microbial infections, pro-inflammatory cytokines, and stress.

2. Inflammatory Diseases: Chronic activation of NF-κB is associated with inflammatory diseases such as rheumatoid arthritis, inflammatory bowel disease (Crohn's disease and ulcerative colitis), and psoriasis.

3. Autoimmune Diseases: Improper regulation of NF-κB can lead to autoimmune diseases, where the immune system mistakenly attacks the body's own tissues. This is due to the overproduction of pro-inflammatory cytokines and other immune mediators.

4. Therapeutic Target: NF-κB is a potential therapeutic target for treating autoimmune and inflammatory diseases. Inhibitors of NF-κB signaling are being explored as potential treatments to reduce inflammation and immune responses.

Once in the nucleus, NF-κB binds to specific DNA sequences and initiates the transcription of target genes involved in inflammation and immune responses. And it may never stop, even when the offending agent is removed!

Such as in:

- **Rheumatoid Arthritis (RA):** NF-κB activation in fibroblast-like synoviocytes (FLS) contributes to the inflammatory picture of RA. These cells produce inflammatory mediators, including cytokines and matrix metalloproteinases, which result in joint and cartilage erosion.

- **Inflammatory Bowel Disease (IBD):** NF-κB signaling plays a role in the pathogenesis of IBD by regulating the expression of cytokines and chemokines involved in inflammation.

NF-κB (nuclear factor kappa-light-chain-enhancer of activated B cells) can be elevated by various stimuli that activate the NF-κB signaling pathway. Here are some common factors that can elevate NF-κB:

1. Infections: Bacterial and viral infections can activate NF-κB as part of the immune response.

2. Cytokines: Pro-inflammatory cytokines such as TNF-α, IL-1β, and IL-6 can activate NF-κB.

3. Oxidative Stress: Reactive oxygen species (ROS) generated during oxidative stress can activate NF-κB.

4. Ultraviolet (UV) Irradiation: Exposure to UV light can lead to NF-κB activation.

5. Heavy Metals: Certain heavy metals, such as cadmium and mercury, can activate NF-κB.

6. Lipopolysaccharides (LPS): Components of the outer membrane of Gram-negative bacteria can trigger NF-κB activation.

7. Growth Factors: Some growth factors, such as TNF-related apoptosis-inducing ligand (TRAIL), can activate NF-κB.

These factors can lead to the activation of NF-κB, which then translocates to the nucleus and promotes the expression of genes involved in inflammation, immune responses, and cell survival. Or death.

Apoptosis is a form of programmed cell death that occurs in a controlled and regulated manner. It is a vital process in maintaining tissue homeostasis eliminating damaged or unwanted cells, and is characterized by specific cellular changes such as cell shrinkage, DNA fragmentation, and membrane blebbing. It is associated with NFKB.

However, certain nutrients and supplements can influence apoptosis and inflammation in the body:

Anti-inflammatory Nutrients

1. Curcumin: Found in turmeric, curcumin has strong anti-inflammatory properties and can help regulate apoptosis.

2. Omega-3 Fatty Acids: Found in fish oil, omega-3 fatty acids (EPA and DHA) have anti-inflammatory effects and can influence cell death pathways.

3. Vitamin D: Adequate levels of vitamin D are important for immune function and may help regulate apoptosis.

4. Zinc: Zinc plays a role in immune function and can influence apoptosis and inflammation.

Interestingly, recent research has shown that zinc can inhibit caspase activity, particularly caspase-1, which is involved in inflammasome activation. Zinc supplementation has been found to alleviate inflammasome-related diseases such as sepsis, **psoriasis, and Alzheimer's disease**. A typical dose is **50 mg per day** of zinc gluconate.

Zinc homeostasis regulates caspase activity and inflammasome activation | PLOS Pathogens

Antioxidants

1. Vitamin C: An antioxidant that can help reduce oxidative stress and inflammation.

2. Vitamin E: Another antioxidant that supports cell membrane integrity and can modulate apoptosis.

Why is this important? Because anything that increases inflammation basically increases apoptosis. You want this amount to be minimal, especially in MS, Parkinson's, or Alzheimer's. These are progressive diseases, and they always beat current medicine.

5. Immune System Modulation:

- **Autoimmune protocol (AIP)**: This is a more restrictive version of the paleo diet that eliminates potential autoimmune triggers, like gluten, dairy, legumes, nightshades, and certain seeds and nuts. It's designed to reduce inflammation and promote immune regulation.

- **Curcumin and other anti-inflammatory herbs**: Curcumin (from turmeric), along with ginger, Boswellia, and green tea extract, can help modulate immune responses and reduce inflammation.

- **Omega-3 fatty acids**: These are anti-inflammatory and can help support immune system balance. They are found in fatty fish (like salmon) and flaxseeds.

- **GSH, preferable in liposomal form**

6. Stress Management:

- **Mind-body practices**: Reducing stress through practices like yoga, meditation, and mindfulness can have a significant impact on autoimmune diseases like Hashimoto's, as stress can exacerbate inflammation and immune system dysfunction.

- **Sleep optimization**: Ensuring quality sleep is vital, as poor sleep can increase cortisol levels, worsening autoimmune conditions. Practices like a consistent sleep schedule, reducing screen time before bed, and creating a restful environment are recommended.

7. Detoxification:

- **Liver support**: The liver is crucial for detoxification, and functional medicine may recommend liver-supporting supplements like milk thistle or dandelion root to aid in toxin removal.

- **Sauna therapy**: Regular use of saunas can help promote sweating, which may assist in eliminating heavy metals and other toxins from the body.

- **Hydration**: Drinking plenty of water and using methods like dry brushing or Epsom salt baths can help support the body's natural detoxification processes.

8. Targeting Underlying Infections:

- **Chronic infections**: Some functional medicine practitioners focus on identifying chronic infections that could trigger autoimmune responses, such as Epstein-Barr virus (EBV), Candida, or gut infections. Addressing these infections with herbs or antimicrobials may be part of the treatment.

9. Lifestyle Factors:

- **Exercise**: Regular, moderate exercise, such as walking, swimming, or yoga, is beneficial for immune health and thyroid function. Intense, high-impact workouts may be counterproductive due to their stress-inducing effects on the body.

- **Weight management**: Maintaining a healthy weight is often part of the overall strategy to manage Hashimoto's, as thyroid dysfunction can impact metabolism.

10. Lab Testing and Monitoring:

- Functional medicine practitioners typically focus on comprehensive lab testing to identify nutrient deficiencies, gut imbalances, heavy metal toxicity, and hormonal imbalances. Common tests may include:
  - Thyroid antibodies (TPO, TgAb)
  - TSH, Free T4, Free T3, Reverse T3 and Glutathione levels
  - Vitamin D, Selenium, Zinc, Iron, B12 levels
  - Gut health testing (e.g., stool analysis)
  - Heavy metal toxicity testing, esp. Bromine, Chloride and Fluoride

1. IBS (Irritable Bowel Syndrome) Functional Medicine Protocols

IBS is a functional gastrointestinal disorder characterized by symptoms like abdominal pain, bloating, and changes in bowel habits. Functional medicine focuses on gut health, food sensitivities, and gut-brain interactions.

Key Strategies:

- **Gut Health Optimization:**

    o **Elimination Diet**: Identify and eliminate common food triggers like gluten, dairy, FODMAPs, soy, and refined sugars.

    o **Low FODMAP Diet**: In cases of IBS, especially IBS-D (diarrhea) and IBS-C (constipation), a low-FODMAP diet can help reduce symptoms.

    o **Probiotics**: Use high-quality probiotics to restore balance to gut microbiota. Strains like *Lactobacillus* and *Bifidobacterium* are commonly used.

    o **Digestive Enzymes**: Supplementation with digestive enzymes (e.g., lipase, amylase, protease) can help improve digestion and nutrient absorption.

    o **Prebiotics**: Foods rich in prebiotics (e.g., garlic, onions, bananas) help nourish beneficial gut bacteria.

    o **Gastrointestinal Repair**: If leaky gut is suspected, use gut-healing supplements such as L-glutamine, zinc, and aloe vera.

- **Stress Management**: Stress can exacerbate IBS symptoms by affecting gut motility and increasing gut permeability. Techniques such as yoga, meditation, or mindfulness can be used to reduce stress.

- **Food Sensitivity Testing**: Functional medicine may recommend testing for sensitivities to common allergens such as gluten, dairy, and soy.

- **Addressing Dysbiosis**: If there is an imbalance in the gut microbiota (e.g., overgrowth of harmful bacteria or yeast), antimicrobials such as herbal formulas (e.g., oregano oil, berberine) may be used.

- (See also SIBO protocols)

2. Diabetes Functional Medicine Protocols

Diabetes, particularly Type 2 diabetes, is a metabolic disorder that results in high blood sugar levels. Functional medicine approaches target insulin resistance, inflammation, and lifestyle factors to manage and even reverse the condition.

Here are some medical papers that discuss the relationship between **gluten and diabetes:**

1. Dietary gluten and type 1 diabetes - The BMJ explored the potential association between maternal gluten intake during pregnancy and the risk of type 1 diabetes in offspring. The article highlights the need for large-scale prospective studies to confirm this association.

2. Adherence to the Gluten-Free Diet: The Key to Improve Glucose Control in Pediatric Subjects with Type 1 Diabetes and Celiac Disease - This paper from SSRN discusses how adherence to a gluten-free diet can improve glucose control in pediatric subjects with both type 1 diabetes and celiac disease. The study compares continuous glucose monitoring metrics in youths with both conditions to those with type 1 diabetes only.

3. The Role of Gluten in Celiac Disease and Type 1 Diabetes - This review article from MDPI examines the comorbid occurrence of celiac disease and type 1 diabetes and explores the current evidence for the role of gluten in both conditions. It discusses the effect of gluten on the immune system and gut microbiota.

The Role of Gluten in Celiac Disease and Type 1 Diabetes

Celiac.com 01/15/2024 - Celiac disease is a chronic autoimmune condition primarily affecting the small intestine due to gluten sensitivity. Celiac disease exhibits various extraintestinal features, with the pancreas being one of the affected organs.

Grains for Type 2 Diabetes?

SOME CURRENT STUDIES SHOW 150 g of whole grains actually decrease chance of diabetes 2

"Higher consumption of total whole grains and several commonly eaten whole grain foods, including whole grain breakfast cereal, oatmeal, dark bread, brown rice, added bran, and wheat germ, was significantly associated with a lower risk of type 2 diabetes. These findings provide further support for the current recommendations of increasing whole grain consumption as part of a healthy diet for the prevention of type 2 diabetes."

Intake of whole grain foods and risk of type 2 diabetes: results from three prospective cohort studies | The BMJ

Whole-Grain Processing and Glycemic Control in Type 2 Diabetes: A Randomized Crossover Trial | Diabetes Care | American Diabetes Association

Key Strategies:

- **Dietary Changes:**

    o **Low-Carb, High-Fiber Diet**: A low-carb diet with a focus on high-quality, non-starchy vegetables, lean proteins, and healthy fats (e.g., olive oil and avocado) can help manage blood sugar levels.

    o **Intermittent Fasting**: Some practitioners recommend intermittent fasting (e.g., 16-hour fasting window) to improve insulin sensitivity and promote weight loss.

    o **Avoid Processed Foods and Sugars**: Minimize or eliminate refined sugars and processed foods, which can spike blood sugar levels.

    o **Anti-inflammatory Foods**: Incorporate foods that help reduce inflammation, such as omega-3 fatty acids (e.g., fatty fish, flaxseeds) and antioxidants (e.g., berries, dark leafy greens).

- **Insulin Sensitivity Support:**

    o **Chromium, Magnesium, and Zinc**: Supplements like chromium picolinate, magnesium, and zinc may support insulin function and improve blood sugar regulation.

    o **Berberine**: A herb shown to help lower blood sugar levels by increasing insulin sensitivity and supporting liver function.

    o **Alpha-Lipoic Acid**: A powerful antioxidant that may improve insulin sensitivity and reduce diabetic neuropathy symptoms.

    o **Berberine**

    o **Cinnamon**

- **Exercise and Movement**: Regular physical activity, including strength training and aerobic exercises, helps improve insulin sensitivity and supports metabolic health.

- **Gut Health**: Dysbiosis (imbalanced gut bacteria) can impact blood sugar levels. Probiotics and a healthy gut microbiome are important for insulin sensitivity.

- **Stress Reduction**: Chronic stress leads to elevated cortisol, which can impair insulin sensitivity and contribute to high blood sugar. Techniques like mindfulness and deep breathing exercises can reduce stress. Play 8 hr YouTube subliminal videos while sleeping. If you grind your teeth at night, waves, rain, or cricket sounds can help your nighttime unconscious stressors.

- **Berberine** is often used as a natural alternative to metformin for managing blood sugar levels. While specific dosages can vary, studies and experts commonly recommend **500 mg to 1500 mg per day**, divided into two or three doses. This dosage has been shown to effectively regulate blood sugar and improve insulin sensitivity, similar to metformin. Some studies suggest it is superior to Metformin. While berberine is sometimes referred to as "nature's Ozempic," this is more of a marketing term than a scientific classification.

Natural TNF and IL-17 blockers can help manage autoimmune diabetes:

Here are some natural options that may help reduce TNF and IL-17 levels:

1. Turmeric (Curcumin): As mentioned earlier, curcumin has anti-inflammatory properties and can inhibit TNF and IL-17 production.

2. Omega-3 Fatty Acids: Found in fish oil, omega-3s have anti-inflammatory effects and can help reduce TNF levels.

3. Green Tea Extract (EGCG): EGCG has been shown to inhibit TNF production and reduce inflammation.

4. Probiotics: Certain probiotics can help balance the gut microbiome and reduce inflammation, potentially lowering TNF and IL-17 levels.

5. Resveratrol: Found in grapes and red wine, resveratrol has anti-inflammatory properties and can inhibit TNF production. But most products are crap!

Resveratrol has a relatively high absorption rate through the small intestine. However, its bioavailability (how much actually gets into the bloodstream) can be quite low due to rapid metabolism and clearance from the body. (Less than 2%).

Micronized resveratrol has been shown to significantly increase absorption. Studies indicate a four-fold increase in plasma concentration with micronized resveratrol.

3. Lupus Functional Medicine Protocols

Lupus is an autoimmune disease that affects multiple organs, including the skin, kidneys, joints, and heart. Functional medicine for lupus focuses on immune system regulation, reducing inflammation, and supporting overall well-being.

Key Strategies:

- **Anti-Inflammatory Diet:**

    o **Gluten-Free, Dairy-Free**: Some lupus patients may have sensitivities to gluten and dairy, which can trigger flare-ups. An elimination diet is commonly recommended.

    o **Carnivore diet**:

    o **Mediterranean Diet**: Rich in healthy fats, fruits, vegetables, and lean proteins, which are anti-inflammatory and promote immune health.

    o **Omega-3 Fatty Acids**: Supplements such as fish oil or krill oil can help reduce inflammation and support immune function.

    o **Avoid Nightshades**: Some patients may find that nightshades (e.g., tomatoes, peppers, eggplant) can worsen inflammation.

- **NOT Ketogenic Diet**: While the keto diet may help reduce inflammation in some cases, its high-fat content could pose risks for individuals with lupus, especially if they have kidney involvement or cardiovascular concerns. More research is needed to determine its safety and effectiveness for lupus.

- **Supplementation:**

    o **Vitamin D3**: Low vitamin D levels are common in lupus and may worsen symptoms. Vitamin D supplementation can help modulate the immune response.

    o **Curcumin and Boswellia**: These herbs have anti-inflammatory properties that may help reduce systemic inflammation in lupus.

    o **Probiotics**: Beneficial bacteria in the gut can help regulate the immune system and reduce inflammation.

Resveratrol shows promise as a complementary therapy for **systemic lupus erythematosus (SLE)** due to its **anti-inflammatory and immune-modulating properties.** Research suggests that resveratrol may help by:

- **Reducing Inflammation**: It inhibits inflammatory pathways, which are often overactive in lupus.

- **Modulating Immune Response**: Resveratrol can help regulate immune cells, potentially reducing the autoimmune attack on healthy tissues.

- **Protecting Organs**: Its antioxidant properties may protect against organ damage caused by lupus-related inflammation.

- Typical doses range from **150 mg to 500 mg daily**.

- **Stress Management**: As stress can exacerbate autoimmune conditions, practices like yoga, mindfulness, and acupuncture may be used to reduce flare-ups.

- **Addressing Leaky Gut and Dysbiosis**: Some lupus patients have gut permeability issues that trigger immune responses. Functional medicine may involve strategies to heal the gut with supplements like L-glutamine and herbs such as marshmallow root.

- **Detoxification**: The liver plays a key role in detoxifying the body, and supporting its function can help reduce the toxic load that may contribute to lupus flare-u

4. Psoriasis Functional Medicine Protocols

Psoriasis is a chronic autoimmune condition characterized by the rapid turnover of skin cells, resulting in thick, scaly patches on the skin. Functional medicine targets inflammation, immune system modulation, and lifestyle interventions to manage psoriasis.

Key Strategies:

- **Anti-Inflammatory Diet:**

  - **Elimination Diet**: Avoid common triggers such as gluten, dairy, processed foods, and sugar.

  - **Omega-3 Fatty Acids**: High doses of omega-3 fatty acids (e.g., from fish oil or flaxseeds) may reduce skin inflammation.

  - **Low Glycemic Index Foods**: Low-GI foods help stabilize blood sugar levels and reduce inflammation.

  - **Antioxidants**: Foods rich in antioxidants, such as berries, dark leafy greens, and cruciferous vegetables, can help combat oxidative stress and inflammation.

- **Nutrient Support:**

  - **Vitamin D3**: Psoriasis is often associated with low levels of vitamin D. Supplementing with vitamin D can help support skin health and immune function.

  - **Zinc**: Zinc plays a role in skin healing and immune regulation. Zinc supplementation may benefit psoriasis patients.

  - **Probiotics**: A healthy gut microbiome can influence skin health, so probiotics may help regulate immune responses that lead to psoriasis flare-ups.

- **Stress Reduction**: Stress is a significant trigger for psoriasis flare-ups. Practices like mindfulness meditation, yoga, and deep breathing exercises can help reduce stress and manage symptoms.

- **Topical Support**: In addition to internal treatments, topical therapies like aloe vera gel, coconut oil, or tea tree oil may help soothe skin irritation and reduce inflammation.

- **Detoxification**: Psoriasis may be linked to toxin buildup in the body. Functional medicine may include liver detox protocols to support toxin elimination, using supplements like milk thistle and dandelion root.

- **Sleep Optimization**: Adequate sleep is crucial for immune regulation and skin health, so ensuring quality rest is an important part of managing psoriasis.

Artichokes have potential benefits for psoriasis and biofilm clearing:

1. Psoriasis: Artichokes are rich in antioxidants like cynarin and silymarin, which support liver detoxification and reduce inflammation. Since psoriasis is linked to inflammation and immune system dysfunction, artichokes may help manage symptoms by promoting overall health and reducing inflammatory markers.

2. Biofilm Clearing: Artichokes contain phenolic compounds that may disrupt biofilms, which are protective layers formed by bacteria. These compounds can help in breaking down biofilms and improving the effectiveness of antimicrobial treatments.

Here are some **effective biofilm disruptors** that can help break down biofilms in the body:

Top Biofilm Disruptors

1. N-Acetylcysteine (NAC) – A powerful antioxidant that helps dissolve biofilms and enhances antimicrobial treatments. 600 mg twice a day, 30 days.

2. Serrapeptase – A systemic enzyme that supports gut, respiratory, and sinus health by breaking down biofilms. The typical **adult dosage** of serrapeptase is **10 mg, taken three times daily** (maximum dose: **60 mg/day**). It's usually recommended to take it **on an empty stomach**, about **2 hours after meals**. Up to **4 weeks**.

Since serrapeptase can interact with **blood-thinning medications**, it's best to consult a healthcare professional before starting.

(These disruptors are commonly used in protocols for **SIBO (Small Intestinal Bacterial Overgrowth), Candida infections, and chronic bacterial issues**.)

Psoriasis Functional Medicine Protocols

Psoriasis is a chronic autoimmune condition characterized by the rapid turnover of skin cells, resulting in thick, scaly patches on the skin. Functional medicine targets inflammation, immune system modulation, and lifestyle interventions to manage psoriasis.

- **Key Strategies:**
- **Anti-Inflammatory Diet:**
- **Elimination Diet:** Avoid common triggers such as gluten, dairy, processed foods, and sugar.

- **Omega-3 Fatty Acids:** High doses of omega-3 fatty acids (e.g., from fish oil or flaxseeds) may reduce skin inflammation.

- **Low Glycemic Index Foods:** Low-GI foods help stabilize blood sugar levels and reduce inflammation.

- **Antioxidants:** Foods rich in antioxidants, such as berries, dark leafy greens, and cruciferous vegetables, can help combat oxidative stress and inflammation.

- **Nutrient Support:**

- **Vitamin D3:** Psoriasis is often associated with low levels of vitamin D. Supplementing with vitamin D can help support skin health and immune function.

- **Zinc:** Zinc plays a role in skin healing and immune regulation. Zinc supplementation may benefit psoriasis patients.

1. **Probiotics:** A healthy gut microbiome can influence skin health, so probiotics may help regulate immune responses that lead to psoriasis flare-ups.

2. **Lactobacillus rhamnosus GG** - Known for its anti-inflammatory properties and ability to modulate immune responses.

3. **Bifidobacterium longum** - Helps reduce gut inflammation and supports a healthy immune system.

4. **Lactobacillus plantarum** - May help decrease pro-inflammatory cytokines, including IL-17.

5. **Saccharomyces boulardii** - A beneficial yeast that supports gut health and reduces inflammation.

These probiotics are often used in managing conditions like **inflammatory bowel disease (IBD)**, **autoimmune disorders**, and other inflammatory conditions

Resveratrol shows promise as a complementary therapy for **systemic lupus erythematosus (SLE)** due to its **anti-inflammatory and immune-modulating properties.** Research suggests that resveratrol may help by:

- **Reducing Inflammation**: It inhibits inflammatory pathways, which are often overactive in lupus.

- **Modulating Immune Response**: Resveratrol can help regulate immune cells, potentially reducing the autoimmune attack on healthy tissues.

- **Protecting Organs**: Its antioxidant properties may protect against organ damage caused by lupus-related inflammation.

- Typical doses range from **150 mg to 500 mg daily**,

- **Curcumin:** Found in turmeric, curcumin has anti-inflammatory properties and can help reduce IL-17 and IL-22 levels

- **Ursolic Acid:** Found in apple peels, ursolic acid has been shown to suppress IL-17 production] (https://www.inspire.com/groups/psoriasis-community/discussion/ursolic-acid-suppress-il-17/). These supplements typically contain doses ranging from **150 mg to 450 mg** per day.

- **Green Tea Extract (EGCG):** Epigallocatechin gallate (EGCG) in green tea has anti-inflammatory effects and may help reduce IL-17 levels]

SIBO

Small Intestinal Bacterial Overgrowth (SIBO)

Common Symptoms

- **Bloating**: A feeling of fullness or swelling in the abdomen, often after meals.

- **Gas**: Excessive flatulence or burping.

- **Abdominal Pain**: Cramping or discomfort in the stomach area.

- **Diarrhea or Constipation**: Irregular bowel movements, sometimes alternating between the two.

- **Nausea**: A queasy feeling, especially after eating.

- **Fatigue**: Feeling tired due to poor nutrient absorption.

- **Unintentional Weight Loss**: Caused by malabsorption of nutrients.

- **Malnutrition**: Deficiencies in vitamins like B12 or fat-soluble vitamins (A, D, E, K).

SIBO can also lead to **changes in stool**, such as oily or floating stools, due to fat malabsorption. If left untreated, it may contribute to long-term issues like **vitamin deficiencies** or **bone health problems**.

Breath Test: Measures hydrogen or methane levels in your breath after consuming a sugar solution (like glucose or lactulose). Elevated levels indicate bacterial overgrowth

IBS Herbal Treatments

1. Oregano Oil

- **Properties:** Oregano oil has potent antimicrobial properties, making it effective against a wide range of bacteria, fungi, and parasites.

- **Usage:** Typically taken in capsule form, with a common dosage being 200 mg 2-3 times daily. It can also be used as an essential oil diluted in water, but this is less common for internal use.

2. Berberine

- **Properties:** Found in herbs like goldenseal, barberry, and Oregon grape root, berberine has strong antibacterial and antifungal properties. It's particularly effective against hydrogen-producing bacteria.

- **Usage:** Often taken as a supplement, with a typical dosage of 500 mg 2-3 times daily. It's best taken with meals.

3. Garlic (Allicin)

- **Properties:** Allicin, the active compound in garlic, has broad-spectrum antimicrobial effects. It's especially effective against methane-producing bacteria.

- **Usage:** Garlic supplements standardized for allicin content are available, with a common dosage being 600-1200 mg per day.

4. Olive Leaf Extract

- **Properties:** Olive leaf extract contains oleuropein, which has antimicrobial and anti-inflammatory properties. It can help combat bacterial overgrowth and support immune health.

- **Usage:** Typically taken in capsule or liquid form, with dosages varying based on concentration. A common dosage is 500-1000 mg per day.

Dietary Changes: Incorporating a low FODMAP diet or specific carbohydrate diet (SCD) can help reduce symptoms and support the effectiveness of herbal treatments.

Lyme disease, caused by the *Borrelia* bacteria and transmitted through tick bites, can lead to a range of symptoms, including fatigue, joint pain, neurological issues, and immune dysregulation. In functional and integrative medicine, treatment for Lyme often involves a multi-faceted approach that goes beyond antibiotics.

Listed are some of the best alternative treatments and herbs for Lyme disease:

1. Herbal Protocols for Lyme Disease

A. Antimicrobial Herbs

Andrographis (Andrographis paniculata): Known as a powerful antimicrobial herb with anti-inflammatory properties. It has been used to fight infections and modulate immune responses. Some studies have shown it to be effective against Lyme disease.

- **Japanese Knotweed (Polygonum cuspidatum)**: Rich in resveratrol, this herb has been widely studied for its ability to help treat Lyme disease. It is thought to have antibacterial properties and may help to reduce inflammation and pain.

- **Cat's Claw (Uncaria tomentosa)**: Known for its immune-boosting and anti-inflammatory effects, Cat's Claw may help combat Lyme disease bacteria, especially in its chronic form.

- **Garlic (Allium sativum)**: Garlic has broad-spectrum antimicrobial properties and is commonly used to fight infections. It has also been found to support immune health.

- **Oregano Oil (Origanum vulgare)**: Oregano oil has strong antimicrobial and antifungal properties. It's sometimes used to help manage chronic infections, including Lyme disease.

B. Immune-Boosting Herbs

These herbs help strengthen the immune system, supporting the body's ability to fight off the Lyme infection and other co-infections often associated with Lyme disease.

- **Echinacea (Echinacea purpurea)**: Echinacea is widely used for its immune-stimulating effects. It can help enhance the body's natural defense against bacterial and viral infections.

- **Astragalus (Astragalus membranaceus)**: Known for its ability to enhance the immune system and fight viral infections, Astragalus also helps protect the body from the damage caused by Lyme disease and its co-infections.

- **Reishi Mushroom (Ganoderma lucidum)**: Reishi is known for its immune-regulating effects and anti-inflammatory properties. It is often used to enhance the immune system and help the body adapt to chronic illness.

- **Elderberry (Sambucus nigra)**: This herb is rich in antioxidants and has been shown to modulate the immune system and help fight infections.

Here are some general dosage guidelines for the herbs commonly used in Lyme disease management:

- **Andrographis**: Typically **400-800 mg** per day, divided into two doses.

- **Japanese Knotweed**: **500-1000 mg** per day, often taken in divided doses.

- **Cat's Claw**: **500-1000 mg** per day, though some protocols use higher amounts.

- **Garlic**: **600-1200 mg** per day (or 1-2 fresh cloves).

- **Oregano Oil**: **1-2 drops** diluted in water or carrier oil, taken **1-3 times daily**.

- **Echinacea**: **300-500 mg** per day or **2-3 mL** of tincture.

- **Astragalus**: **500-1000 mg** per day, often used for immune support.

- **Reishi Mushroom**: **1000-3000 mg** per day, depending on the extract form.

- **Elderberry (Sambucus nigra) 600 per day**

C. Anti-inflammatory and Pain-Relieving Herbs

Lyme disease often causes inflammation and pain in the joints, muscles, and nervous system. These herbs can help reduce these symptoms.

- **Turmeric (Curcuma longa)**: Curcumin, the active compound in turmeric, is a potent anti-inflammatory agent that may help manage the pain and inflammation associated with Lyme disease. Find one that has black pepper in it for better absorption.

- **Boswellia (Boswellia serrata)**: Known for its anti-inflammatory effects, Boswellia may help reduce inflammation in joints and tissues, which is common in Lyme disease.

- **Devil's Claw (Harpagophytum procumbens)**: Often used to manage pain and inflammation, especially in musculoskeletal conditions, Devil's Claw can help reduce the pain and stiffness associated with Lyme disease.

D. Detoxifying Herbs

These herbs support the body's detoxification processes, helping to clear out toxins that may be released as the Lyme infection is addressed.

- **Milk Thistle (Silybum marianum)**: Milk Thistle is a liver-supportive herb that helps detoxify the body. It can be especially useful in clearing out toxins and supporting the detoxification of the liver, which is essential when dealing with Lyme.

- **Dandelion Root (Taraxacum officinale)**: Known for its detoxifying effects on the liver and kidneys, dandelion root may help eliminate waste products and toxins that accumulate during an infection.

Here are general dosage guidelines for these herbs:

Anti-inflammatory and Pain-Relieving Herbs

- **Turmeric (Curcuma longa)**: **500-2000 mg** per day of curcumin extract, often taken with black pepper (piperine) to enhance absorption.

- **Boswellia (Boswellia serrata)**: **300-500 mg** of standardized extract **2-3 times daily**.

- **Devil's Claw (Harpagophytum procumbens)**: **500-1000 mg** per day, often divided into two doses.

Detoxifying Herbs

- **Milk Thistle (Silybum marianum):** 300-600 mg per day of standardized extract containing 70-80% silymarin.

- **Dandelion Root (Taraxacum officinale):** 500-1500 mg per day or 1-2 cups of tea daily.

2. Dietary and Lifestyle Support

- **Anti-Inflammatory Diet**: A diet rich in anti-inflammatory foods (e.g., vegetables, healthy fats, omega-3s, lean proteins) and low in processed foods and sugars can help reduce inflammation, improve immune function, and support healing.

- **Gut Health**: Supporting gut health is crucial since Lyme disease and its treatment can disrupt the gut microbiome. Probiotics, prebiotics, and foods that promote gut health can help maintain a healthy gut barrier, reduce systemic inflammation, and enhance the body's ability to fight infections.

- **Sleep Hygiene**: Adequate and restful sleep is essential for recovery, as it supports the immune system and reduces inflammation. Practicing good sleep hygiene and managing stress is a key component of any Lyme treatment plan.

3. Mind-Body Techniques

Chronic Lyme disease often leads to mental and emotional stress. Managing this stress can be crucial for recovery.

- **Meditation and Mindfulness**: These practices can help reduce stress, calm the nervous system, and support overall well-being.

- **Yoga**: Gentle yoga can help relieve muscle tension, reduce stress, and improve circulation. It can also support joint health, which is important for people with Lyme disease.

- **Acupuncture**: Acupuncture can help alleviate pain, reduce inflammation, and improve circulation. Some practitioners use acupuncture as part of an integrated Lyme disease treatment plan.

Medications for Lyme Disease (Besides Doxycycline)

While **doxycycline** is the first-line treatment for Lyme disease, especially in the early stages, there are other medications used depending on the patient's condition, age, or other factors

1. Alternative Antibiotics for Lyme Disease:

- **Amoxicillin:**

    o **Indication**: Used in cases where doxycycline is not suitable, such as for pregnant women or children under 8 years old.

    o **Mechanism**: Like doxycycline, amoxicillin targets the bacteria causing Lyme disease, but it is often preferred for pediatric patients.

- **Cefuroxime axetil (Ceftin):**

    o **Indication**: Another option for those who cannot tolerate doxycycline. It is used for patients with Lyme disease that has affected the central nervous system (CNS) or those with more complex cases.

    o **Mechanism**: A second-generation cephalosporin antibiotic that is effective against *Borrelia* species.

- **Ceftriaxone (Rocephin):**

    o **Indication**: Used in more severe cases of Lyme disease, particularly when the infection affects the CNS or other organ systems, such as in **neuroborreliosis** (Lyme-related neurological disease).

    o **Administration**: Usually given intravenously (IV) in hospital settings for more serious infections, including those with complications like meningitis or encephalitis.

- **Azithromycin (Zithromax):**

    o **Indication**: This macrolide antibiotic is sometimes used in combination with other antibiotics to treat Lyme disease, especially in patients who have allergies or intolerances to other antibiotics.

    o **Mechanism**: It works by inhibiting bacterial protein synthesis, affecting the bacteria's ability to grow and reproduce.

- **Rifampin:**

    o **Indication**: It may be used for Lyme disease with co-infections like **babesiosis** or **bartonellosis**. Rifampin is often prescribed when treating complex cases involving Lyme disease and co-infections.

    o **Mechanism**: Rifampin works by inhibiting bacterial RNA synthesis.

- **Minocycline:**

    o **Indication**: A tetracycline antibiotic that is sometimes used in place of doxycycline, especially for persistent or chronic Lyme disease.

    o **Mechanism**: Similar to doxycycline in terms of its effect on bacteria, but it may be preferred in certain situations due to its better penetration into the tissues.

- **Hydroxychloroquine:**

  - o **Indication**: Sometimes used in conjunction with other medications for Lyme disease, particularly in cases with co-infections like **babesiosis** or **bartonellosis**, or for managing autoimmune-like symptoms resulting from chronic Lyme.

  - o **Mechanism**: Works by inhibiting the ability of the bacteria to survive and reproduce within red blood cells.

Co-Infections from Tick Bites

Ticks, particularly the **Ixodes** species (commonly referred to as black-legged or deer ticks), are vectors for various other infections in addition to Lyme disease. These co-infections complicate the diagnosis and treatment of Lyme disease and can contribute to chronic symptoms.

Common Co-Infections Associated with Tick Bites:

1. Babesiosis:

- **Cause**: A protozoan parasite (*Babesia* species) that infects red blood cells.
- **Symptoms**: Flu-like symptoms, fever, chills, fatigue, muscle aches, and anemia.
- **Treatment**: Often treated with a combination of **atovaquone** and **azithromycin** or **quinine** and **clindamycin**.

2. Anaplasmosis (formerly Ehrlichiosis):

- **Cause**: *Anaplasma phagocytophilum*, a bacterium that infects white blood cells.
- **Symptoms**: Fever, chills, headache, muscle aches, and fatigue, similar to Lyme.
- **Treatment**: Typically treated with **doxycycline** or **rifampin** in more severe cases.

3. Bartonellosis (Cat Scratch Fever):

- **Cause**: Bartonella species, including Bartonella henselae.
- **Symptoms**: Can range from fever, fatigue, and swollen lymph nodes to more severe neurological issues.
- **Treatment**: Often treated with **azithromycin** or **rifampin**, sometimes in combination with other antibiotics.

4. Rocky Mountain Spotted Fever (RMSF):

- **Cause**: *Rickettsia rickettsii*, a bacterium transmitted by ticks.
- **Symptoms**: Fever, rash, headache, and muscle pain. The rash often starts at the wrists and ankles and spreads inward.
- **Treatment**: Treated with **doxycycline** or **chloramphenicol**.

5. Tick-borne Relapsing Fever (TBRF):

- **Cause**: *Borrelia* species distinct from *Borrelia burgdorferi* (which causes Lyme).
- **Symptoms**: Cyclic fevers, headache, muscle pain, and fatigue.
- **Treatment**: Treated with **doxycycline** or **penicillin**.

6. Babesia microti:

- **Cause**: A protozoan parasite that causes babesiosis.
- **Symptoms**: Similar to malaria, causing fever, chills, fatigue, and red blood cell destruction.
- **Treatment**: **Atovaquone** combined with **azithromycin** or **clindamycin** and **quinine**.

7. Tick-Borne Encephalitis (TBE):

- **Cause**: Tick-borne encephalitis virus.
- **Symptoms**: Fever, fatigue, headaches, and neurological symptoms (e.g., meningitis, encephalitis).
- **Treatment**: There is no specific antiviral treatment for TBE, but supportive care (e.g., pain relievers, IV fluids) is important.

Seventh Edition April 2017 of Lyme Disease and associated diseases

CD57 Marker and Lyme Disease

The **CD57** marker is a type of cell surface protein expressed on certain immune cells, including natural killer (NK) cells and some T-cells. In the context of Lyme disease, it is sometimes used as a marker of immune system dysfunction.

Explanation of CD57 in Lyme Disease:

- **CD57 Depletion**: Chronic Lyme disease patients often show a **decrease in CD57** levels. This decrease is linked to immune system dysfunction, as CD57+ NK cells play a role in fighting infections, including Lyme.
- **Clinical Relevance:**

   o **Low CD57 Levels**: A reduction in CD57 levels can suggest a **chronic infection**, including Lyme disease. It may be used as a diagnostic tool or to assess the severity of immune system impairment due to chronic Lyme.

   o **Immune Dysregulation**: Chronic Lyme disease may lead to long-term immune suppression or dysregulation, contributing to persistent symptoms even after treatment with antibiotics. The CD57 marker is sometimes used to monitor disease progression and immune function.

   o **Lyme Disease and Co-Infections**: Low CD57 levels have also been observed in patients with Lyme co-infections, further suggesting a suppressed immune response.

CD57 Testing:

- **CD57 testing** is not universally recommended or validated as a diagnostic tool for Lyme disease, but it is used by some clinicians as part of an integrated approach to assessing chronic Lyme. A **low CD57 count** may be indicative of a chronic infection or the presence of a persistent bacterial load, even in the face of antibiotic treatment.

Interpretation:

- **Normal CD57 count**: Indicates the immune system is likely functioning well.

- **Low CD57 count**: May point to chronic infection, autoimmune conditions, or other persistent inflammatory conditions. In the context of Lyme, it suggests the possibility of ongoing or unresolved infection.

Key Markers and Tests

1. ELISA (Enzyme-Linked Immunosorbent Assay): This test detects antibodies to Borrelia burgdorferi. It's often used as the first step in Lyme disease testing1.

2. Western Blot: This test confirms the presence of antibodies detected by the ELISA test. It's used as a second step to ensure accuracy1.

3. IgM and IgG Antibodies: IgM antibodies are usually the first to appear after infection and indicate recent exposure. IgG antibodies develop later and can indicate a longer-term infection1.

Conclusion:

- **Medications**: Beyond doxycycline, Lyme disease may be treated with other antibiotics like **amoxicillin**, **cefuroxime**, or **ceftriaxone**, depending on the severity and stage of infection.

- **Co-Infections**: Lyme disease is frequently accompanied by other infections such as **babesiosis**, **anaplasmosis**, **bartonellosis**, and **RMSF** that may require additional treatment.

- **CD57 Marker**: A low CD57 count may suggest chronic Lyme disease or other persistent infections, as it reflects immune system dysfunction, which is often seen in patients with long-term Lyme disease.

MULTIPLE sclerosis (MS) is a complex disease, and while there is currently no cure, there have been promising developments in the field of myelin repair. Here are some   key points:

1. Myelin Repair: Research has shown that promoting myelin repair, or remyelination, can potentially reverse some of the damage caused by MS. Myelin is the protective sheath around nerve fibers, and damage to this sheath is a hallmark of MS.

2. Breakthrough Treatments: Recent studies have identified potential treatments that can regenerate myelin. For example, a study published in 2024 found that a small molecule called ESI1 can promote myelin production in mice and lab-prepared human brain cells. This treatment has shown early promise in reversing myelin damage.

3. Ongoing Research: Scientists are continuously exploring new ways to promote myelin repair and regeneration. Some treatments are still in the experimental stage and require further testing to determine their effectiveness and safety in humans. [Breakthrough Treatment Reverses Myelin Damage in Multiple Sclerosis, Study Finds - ScienceBlog.com](https://scienceblog.com)

LONG COVID: Nitric oxide, resveratrol, and glutathione are all substances that I have used for their benefits in various health conditions, including

1. Nitric Oxide (NO)

- **What It Is**: Nitric oxide is a molecule that naturally occurs in the body and plays a crucial role in blood flow, immune function, and reducing inflammation. It helps dilate blood vessels, which improves circulation and oxygen delivery to tissues.

- **Potential Benefits of Long COVID:**

  o **Improved Circulation**: Nitric oxide's ability to enhance blood flow may help individuals dealing with fatigue or cognitive symptoms by improving oxygen delivery to tissues and organs, including the brain.

  o **Respiratory Support**: In some studies, nitric oxide has been shown to help with lung function, especially in patients with respiratory issues, which could benefit individuals experiencing lingering shortness of breath.

  o **Anti-Inflammatory**: Nitric oxide may help reduce the chronic inflammation seen in long COVID.

- **How to Boost Nitric Oxide:**

  o **Diet**: Foods high in nitrates, such as beets, spinach, arugula, and celery, may help boost nitric oxide levels in the body.

  o **Supplements**: Nitric oxide supplements (such as L-arginine or L-citrulline) are sometimes used, but these could increase viral reactions. CAUTION

  o **Make sure you get only a LIPOSOMAL formula**. Nitric oxide (NO) plays a significant role in regulating TH17 cells, which is the start of many autoimmune diseases.

- **The Downside**: it is a vasodilator, lowering blood pressure, but increasing energy.

2. Resveratrol

- **What It Is**: Resveratrol is a polyphenol, a natural compound found in certain plants. It's most commonly known for its presence in red wine, grapes, and some berries. Resveratrol is an antioxidant with anti-inflammatory properties.

- **Potential Benefits of Long COVID:**

  o **Antioxidant and Anti-Inflammatory**: Resveratrol may help reduce oxidative stress and inflammation in the body, which are common issues in long COVID.

  o **Cardiovascular Support**: Long COVID can sometimes lead to cardiovascular issues, and resveratrol may help protect blood vessels and improve circulation, reducing the risk of heart problems.

  o **Neuroprotective Effects**: Some studies suggest that resveratrol may have protective effects on brain health, potentially aiding those with cognitive symptoms like brain fog.

- **Sources**: Resveratrol is found in red grapes, blueberries, raspberries, dark chocolate, and peanuts. It's also available as a supplement.

- **Considerations**: While resveratrol has potential benefits, its effects are still being studied, so it's important to consult with a healthcare provider before using supplements, especially if you're on other medications.

- **It can be given when glutathione is contraindicated, as in some cancers**.

- **Only one product is worth it, by APEX**. The pills are only 2% absorbed!

3. Glutathione (NAC)

- **What It Is**: Glutathione is a powerful antioxidant produced by the body. It plays a critical role in detoxification, reducing oxidative stress, and supporting the immune system. It also helps regenerate other antioxidants and neutralize free radicals.

- **Potential Benefits of Long COVID:**

  - **Immune Support**: Glutathione helps support a healthy immune system, which can be particularly beneficial for individuals recovering from long COVID, as it helps reduce inflammation and may support overall immune function.

  - **Liver Detoxification**: Glutathione is crucial for liver health and detoxification, helping the body clear out toxins, which can be helpful if there's any liver strain from prolonged illness or medications.

  - **Reduction of Fatigue**: Some studies suggest that glutathione supplementation may help with fatigue, one of the most common and debilitating symptoms of long COVID.

  - **Neurological Health**: Due to its antioxidant properties, glutathione may also help protect the brain from oxidative damage and support mental clarity.

Sources: Glutathione is found in foods like spinach, avocado, asparagus, and walnuts. However, glutathione is not well-absorbed through the digestive system, so many people use supplements in the form of liposomal glutathione or precursors like N-acetyl cysteine (NAC) to boost glutathione levels.

N-acetylcysteine (NAC) has been studied for its potential benefits in respiratory health and immune support, including during COVID-19. While there isn't a universally established dosage for COVID-19 prevention, studies and protocols often suggest **600 mg to 1200 mg per day**, divided into two doses, as a general guideline for immune support and antioxidant benefits.

Glutathione is a powerful antioxidant that helps detoxify the body and protect cells from damage. However, its role in cancer is complex and can vary depending on the type of cancer and the individual's overall health.

Some studies suggest that glutathione may protect cancer cells from chemotherapy and radiation therapy by neutralizing the reactive oxygen species (ROS) that these treatments generate to kill cancer cells. This could potentially make cancer treatments less effective.

On the other hand, glutathione is also known to reduce side effects of chemotherapy, such as neutropenia (low white blood cell count) and hepatotoxicity (liver damage). It may also help improve the quality of life for cancer patients by reducing oxidative stress and inflammation.

The oral form of this is comparable to NAC, which many of you read may help reduce COVID at 600 mg 2 x day.

For the MCAS reaction (Histamine) people often get, we can treat it with a DAO supplement.

https://pmc.ncbi.nlm.nih.gov/articles/PMC6859183/

Key Takeaways for Long COVID:

- **Nitric oxide**, **resveratrol**, and **glutathione** all have potential roles in managing long COVID symptoms by addressing inflammation, oxidative stress, and immune function.

- **Also, treats for EBV.**

Maintaining proper nutrition is a crucial part of supporting recovery and managing symptoms. The right nutrients help boost the immune system, reduce inflammation, and address fatigue, brain fog, and other lingering effects.

Here are some key nutrients and dietary recommendations for people dealing with long COVID:

1. Vitamin D3

- **Why It's Important**: Vitamin D plays a key role in immune function, and many people with long COVID have reported low levels of vitamin D. It may also help in reducing inflammation.

- AND vitamin D can indeed influence myostatin levels. Research has shown that high doses of vitamin D can reduce myostatin production, which in turn can lead to increased muscle mass and strength. Myostatin is a protein that inhibits muscle growth, so lowering its levels can be beneficial for muscle development.

- **Sources**: Sunlight (a natural source), fortified foods (like milk or cereals), fatty fish (like salmon, mackerel, or sardines), and egg yolks. Vitamin D supplements might be necessary, but always consult a healthcare provider before starting.

2. Vitamin C

- **Why It's Important**: Vitamin C is a powerful antioxidant that supports immune health, helps fight infection, and reduces inflammation.

- **Sources**: Citrus fruits (oranges, grapefruits), strawberries, kiwi, bell peppers, broccoli, and leafy greens.

3. B Vitamins (B1, B2, B6, B12, Folate)

- **Why It's Important**: B vitamins are vital for energy production, brain function, and reducing fatigue. Low B12 levels have been associated with cognitive symptoms like brain fog.

- **Sources**: Whole grains, eggs, dairy products, legumes, leafy greens, meat, fish, and fortified cereals. A B-complex supplement may be considered if levels are low, but check with a doctor first.

4. Magnesium

- **Why It's Important**: Magnesium is essential for muscle function, relaxation, and reducing fatigue and headaches. It also supports the nervous system and may help with symptoms like insomnia and anxiety.

- **Sources**: Nuts (especially almonds), seeds, leafy greens, whole grains, legumes, and dark chocolate. More in the next few pages.

5. Omega-3 Fatty Acids (EPA & DHA)

- **Why It's Important**: Omega-3 fatty acids have anti-inflammatory properties that may help manage long COVID symptoms, especially those related to inflammation in the body, such as joint pain and fatigue.

- **Sources**: Fatty fish (salmon, sardines), flaxseeds, chia seeds, walnuts, and omega-3 supplements if needed.

6. Zinc

- **Why It's Important**: Zinc supports immune function and plays a role in healing, cell growth, and tissue repair. Zinc deficiency has been linked to increased susceptibility to infections.

- **Sources**: Meat, shellfish, beans, lentils, seeds, nuts, dairy, and whole grains.

7. Protein

- **Why It's Important**: Protein is essential for muscle repair, immune system function, and overall tissue recovery, especially if there's muscle weakness or atrophy from prolonged illness.

- **Sources**: Lean meats, poultry, fish, eggs, dairy, tofu, tempeh, and nuts.

8. Probiotics and Prebiotics

- **Why It's Important**: The gut microbiome plays a crucial role in immune function, and maintaining a healthy gut can help with overall recovery and inflammation management.

- **Sources**: Probiotics can be found in yogurt, kefir, and fermented foods like sauerkraut or kimchi. Prebiotics (fiber-rich foods) include garlic, onions, bananas, oats, and apples.

9. Antioxidants (Flavonoids, Polyphenols)

- **Why It's Important**: Antioxidants help reduce oxidative stress and inflammation, both of which are commonly elevated in long COVID. They may also help with symptoms like fatigue and muscle pain.

- **Sources**: Berries, dark chocolate (in moderation), green tea, apples, onions, and colorful vegetables like carrots and spinach.

10. Iron

- **Why It's Important**: Anemia can occur in long COVID, leading to fatigue and weakness. Iron is essential for red blood cell production and oxygen transport.

- **Sources**: Red meat, poultry, seafood, lentils, beans, tofu, spinach, and fortified cereals. Vitamin C can help with the absorption of plant-based iron.

- Nonetheless, **iron can exacerbate certain autoimmune conditions**. Excess iron in the body can promote inflammation and oxidative stress, which can worsen autoimmune responses. Conditions such as rheumatoid arthritis, systemic lupus erythematosus (lupus), and inflammatory bowel disease can be negatively impacted by iron overload.

General Tips:

- **Eat a Balanced Diet**: Focus on a variety of whole foods to ensure you're getting a range of nutrients.

- **Stay Hydrated**: Drinking plenty of water is essential, especially if you're experiencing fatigue, headaches, or other symptoms that can be worsened by dehydration.

- **Small, Frequent Meals**: If you're dealing with fatigue, try eating smaller, more frequent meals to maintain energy throughout the day without overburdening your system.

Hashimoto's thyroiditis:

Functional medicine focuses on addressing the root causes of diseases and emphasizes holistic, individualized approaches. When it comes to Hashimoto's thyroiditis, which is an autoimmune disorder leading to hypothyroidism, the functional medicine approach involves identifying and addressing underlying factors contributing to the condition. Here are some of the key functional medicine strategies and treatments for Hashimoto's:

1. Nutritional Support:

- **Anti-inflammatory diet**: Focusing on whole foods, including fruits, vegetables, healthy fats (e.g., avocado, olive oil), and high-quality proteins (e.g., grass-fed meat, wild-caught fish).

- **Gluten-free diet**: Since gluten has been associated with autoimmune responses in some individuals, a gluten-free diet is often recommended.

- **Nutrient-dense foods**: Prioritize foods rich in vitamins and minerals, particularly those important for thyroid health, such as:

  - **Iodine**: Necessary for thyroid hormone production, but should be used cautiously as excessive iodine can worsen Hashimoto's.

  - **Selenium**: Found in Brazil nuts, eggs, and fish, selenium is important for the conversion of T4 (inactive thyroid hormone) to T3 (active thyroid hormone).

  - **Zinc**: Supports thyroid function and immune health. Sources include shellfish, pumpkin seeds, and meat.

  - **Vitamin D**: Vitamin D deficiency is common in people with Hashimoto's, and supplementing it can help support immune function.

  - **Magnesium**: Often recommended for its role in thyroid function and overall relaxation.

- **Avoiding goitrogens**: These compounds, found in foods like soy, cruciferous vegetables (e.g., broccoli, cabbage), and cassava, can interfere with iodine absorption and thyroid function when eaten in large amounts.

2. Gut Health Optimization:

- **Leaky gut**: Many autoimmune diseases, including Hashimoto's, are linked to an imbalance in gut health. Repairing the gut lining through diet, probiotics, and addressing food sensitivities is a key strategy in functional medicine.

- **Probiotics**: Incorporating probiotics (e.g., Lactobacillus, Bifidobacterium) can help restore gut flora, supporting immune balance.

- **Digestive enzymes**: Some people with Hashimoto's have digestive issues that may benefit from enzyme supplementation to improve nutrient absorption and reduce inflammation.

3. Addressing Environmental Triggers:

- **Toxin reduction**: Reducing exposure to environmental toxins, such as heavy metals, pesticides, and endocrine-disrupting chemicals, is crucial. Functional medicine practitioners may recommend detox protocols or lifestyle adjustments, such as using non-toxic cleaning products and avoiding plastic containers.

- **Mold exposure**: Mold can trigger autoimmune responses in susceptible individuals, so addressing any mold exposure in the home environment is often a priority.

4. Thyroid Support and Hormonal Balance:

- **Thyroid hormone replacement**: In some cases, functional medicine practitioners recommend using natural desiccated thyroid (NDT) or synthetic thyroid hormone like levothyroxine to correct hormone deficiencies.

- **T3 supplementation**: In some cases, adding T3 (liothyronine) to T4 therapy may be recommended if T4 conversion is impaired.

- **Addressing adrenal health**: The adrenal glands produce cortisol, which helps manage stress. Chronic stress can exacerbate Hashimoto's symptoms. Adaptogens like ashwagandha, Rhodiola, and licorice root may be used to support the adrenal glands and reduce cortisol imbalance.

NAC, selenium, or reduced glutathione to support thyroid detoxification:

DETOXADINE NACENT IODINE. Nascent iodine supplements, like Detoxadine, are primarily used to support thyroid health and hormone balance. They provide iodine in a form that's easily absorbed by the body, which is essential for the thyroid gland to produce hormones.

While the main focus is on thyroid health, iodine also plays a role in detoxification by helping to eliminate harmful halides like fluoride, chlorine, and bromine from the body. However, it's not specifically targeted at gut health.

The iodine patch test is a simple, at-home method to check for iodine deficiency. Here's how to perform it:

1. Purchase Iodine Tincture: Get an orange iodine tincture solution (not the clear one) from a pharmacy.

2. Apply the Iodine: Using a cotton swab, paint a 2-inch by 2-inch square on your inner forearm, abdomen, or inner thigh. Let it dry completely before touching anything, as it can stain.

3. Observe: Check the patch every few hours over the next 24 hours. If the patch is still visible after 24 hours, it suggests normal iodine levels. If it disappears or significantly lightens within 18 hours, it may indicate iodine deficiency.

Keep in mind that this test isn't 100% reliable and doesn't provide a comprehensive view of your iodine levels. For a more accurate assessment, it's best to consider a urine or blood test.

Hypothyroid can occur slowly over time, says Cleveland Clinic:

- Brain fog (forgetfulness or difficulty concentrating).

- Depression and anxiety.

- Dry, coarse skin and hair.

- Elevated blood cholesterol levels.

- Feeling tired (fatigue).

- Frequent or heavy menstrual periods.

- Hoarseness.

- Inability to tolerate cold temperatures.

- Numbness or tingling in your hands.

- Physical changes in your face (drooping eyelids, puffiness around your eyes).

- Soreness or muscle weakness.

- Unexplained weight gain.

Medically, it's listed as incurable. A lifetime of hormone replacement.

Instead of treating the cause, autoimmunity.

And it's not that difficult. Standard T4, T3, and TSH do nothing to prevent it from getting worse, so these blood tests are a joke. TBG ab and TPO, rT3, blood tests have to be run, as well as iodine, selenium, zinc Vit D deficiency, and/or excess chlorine or bromine in your system, which block it. And if your doctor won't order them, online companies like Privatemdlabs.com or Ultalabtests.com will let you run your own panel.

And there is a correlation with celiac diss.

I find Hashimoto is one of the easiest to treat, by fixing the immune system. It is not just a thyroid issue!!! It's time for the endocrinologist to wake up to reality!

If Grave's is suggested, TSI -ab and TRH ab need to be ordered. (Ab = antibody)

Parkinson's disease (PD) and its progression.

1. Homocysteine and PD: Elevated homocysteine levels are associated with increased risk and faster progression of PD. This is because high homocysteine levels can have a deleterious effect on neurons, particularly those affected by PD.

2. Levodopa and Homocysteine: Levodopa, a common medication used to treat PD, can increase homocysteine levels. This is because levodopa is metabolized in the body, leading to the production of homocysteine as a byproduct.

3. Managing Homocysteine Levels: To counteract the increase in homocysteine levels caused by levodopa, patients are often advised to take supplements like vitamin B6, B12, and methyl folate, NOT Folic acid. These vitamins help in the metabolism of homocysteine, reducing its levels in the body.

4. Cognitive Impairment: Elevated homocysteine levels have also been linked to cognitive impairment in PD patients. Studies have shown that higher homocysteine levels are associated with worse cognitive function, particularly in executive functions. Take methylated B vitamins, esp. MTHF (B12)

Frontiers | Association of plasma homocysteine with cognitive impairment in patients with Parkinson's disease

Human bacteria have been shown to produce and/or consume a wide range of mammalian neurotransmitters, including norepinephrine, dopamine, serotonin, and gamma-aminobutyric acid (GABA) (Galland, 2014; Strandwitz, 2018). Human immune cell activity is also modulated by the microbiome/virome-derived proteins and metabolites.

It follows that microbiome/virome dysbiosis can disrupt the homeostasis of host signaling pathways in a manner that might impact chronic disease development. For example, Tetz et al. (2018) identified changes in the Parkinson's disease gut bacteriophage community. These included shifts in the bacteriophage/bacteria ratio of bacteria known to produce dopamine – the neurotransmitter involved in Parkinson's pathology (Masato et al., 2019). There was a depletion of *Lactococcus* spp. in the PD group.

Emerging research suggests that the gut microbiome plays a significant role in Parkinson's disease (PD). Certain beneficial bacteria may help improve gut health and potentially alleviate some symptoms of PD. For example:

- **Short-chain fatty acid-producing bacteria**: These bacteria, such as *Faecalibacterium* and *Roseburia*, are known to modulate inflammation and support gut-brain communication.

Probiotic strains: *Lactobacillus* and *Bifidobacterium* are commonly studied for their potential to improve gut health and reduce gastrointestinal dysfunctions, which are prevalent in PD.

Protein-rich foods: Foods like turkey, beef, eggs, dairy, soy, and legumes contain amino acids like tyrosine and phenylalanine, which are essential for dopamine production.

Additionally, maintaining a healthy diet rich in fiber and fermented foods can support the growth of beneficial gut bacteria.

I add a bottle of APEX Neuroflam every month to minimize the progressive damage to the brain.

Multiple sclerosis (MS) is a complex disease, and while there is currently no cure, there have been promising developments in the field of myelin repair. Here are some key points:

1. Myelin Repair: Research has shown that promoting myelin repair, or remyelination, can potentially reverse some of the damage caused by MS. Myelin is the protective sheath around nerve fibers, and damage to this sheath is a hallmark of MS.

2. Breakthrough Treatments: Recent studies have identified potential treatments that can regenerate myelin. For example, a study published in 2024 found that a small molecule called ESI1 can promote myelin production in mice and lab-prepared human brain cells. This treatment has shown early promise in reversing myelin damage.

<u>Breakthrough Treatment Reverses Myelin Damage in Multiple Sclerosis, Study Finds - ScienceBlog.com</u>

CANCER:

While no single food can be considered a cure, certain foods have been identified for their potential health benefits and their role in disease prevention. Here are some foods that have garnered attention for their potential anticancer properties:

1. Berries: Rich in antioxidants like anthocyanins, berries (such as blueberries, strawberries, and cherries) have been studied for their potential to reduce cancer risk.

2. Cruciferous Vegetables: Vegetables like broccoli, cauliflower, and Brussels sprouts contain compounds like indole-3-carbinol, which may help lower cancer risk.

3. Fish: Oily fish like salmon and tuna are high in omega-3 fatty acids, which have been linked to reduced inflammation and lower cancer risk.

4. Whole Grains: Foods like oats, quinoa, and brown rice are rich in fiber and nutrients that may help protect against cancer. THESE STUDIES ARE FROM 2016. WHERE'S THE NEW DATA???? 2024 Such estimates indicated that consuming whole grains, on average, was related to a 9.9% decreased risk of Ischemic heart disease, a 9.1.% lower risk of Diabetes 2, a 7.0% lower risk of Colorectal cancer, and a 6.4% lower risk of stroke compared to zero-g of whole grain intake.

Liu, H., Zhu, J., Gao, R. *et al.* Estimating effects of whole grain consumption on type 2 diabetes, colorectal cancer, and cardiovascular disease: a burden of proof study. *Nutr J* **23**, 49 (2024). https://doi.org/10.1186/s12937-024-00957-x

1. Fermented Foods: Foods like yogurt, kimchi, and sauerkraut contain probiotics that can support gut health and potentially reduce cancer risk.

With breast cancer, both **resveratrol** and **glutathione** have been studied for their potential benefits, but they work in different ways:

1. Resveratrol: This polyphenol, found in foods like grapes and blueberries, has shown promise in inhibiting breast cancer cell proliferation, reducing metastasis, and enhancing the effectiveness of chemotherapy drugs. Resveratrol's antioxidant and anti-inflammatory properties make it a candidate for both prevention and treatment.

2. Glutathione: Known as the body's "master antioxidant," glutathione plays a dual role in cancer. While it helps detoxify carcinogens and protect healthy cells, elevated glutathione levels in cancer cells can contribute to treatment resistance. Targeting glutathione metabolism is being explored as a strategy to make cancer cells more susceptible to therapies.

Rheumatoid Arthritis (RA:

1. Anti-Inflammatory Diet

- **Elimination Diet**: Remove potential triggers like gluten, dairy, and processed foods.
- **Omega-3 Fatty Acids**: Found in fish oil supplements (2-4 grams daily) to reduce joint inflammation.

2. Gut Health Support

- **Probiotics**: Strains like *Lactobacillus rhamnosus* and *Bifidobacterium longum* (10-20 billion CFUs daily).
- **Glutamine**: Supports gut lining integrity (5 grams daily).

3. Targeted Supplements

- **Curcumin**: Anti-inflammatory compound from turmeric (500-1000 mg, 2-3 times daily).
- **Vitamin D**: Supports immune regulation (2000-5000 IU daily, based on blood levels).
- **Magnesium**: Reduces muscle tension and inflammation (200-400 mg daily).
- **Boswellia Serrata**: Herbal extract for joint health (300-500 mg, 2-3 times daily).

4. Lifestyle Modifications

- **Stress Management**: Practices like yoga or meditation to reduce stress-induced inflammation.
- **Low-Impact Exercise**: Activities like swimming or walking to maintain joint mobility.

A product called Penetrex is great for local inflammation. Available everywhere.

Fibromyalgia and atlanto-occipital misalignment are two conditions that can significantly impact your health.

Similar to low thyroid or EBV, Fibromyalgia is a chronic condition characterized by widespread musculoskeletal pain, fatigue, and tenderness in localized areas. Patients often experience numerous other symptoms, such as sleep disturbances, headaches, and cognitive difficulties, which are often referred to as "fibro fog."

Atlanto-occipital misalignment or upper cervical spine misalignment involves the misalignment of the first cervical vertebra (the atlas) and the base of the skull (the occiput). This misalignment can lead to muscle tension, chronic pain, and may affect the biomechanics of the spine. It can stem from various causes, including trauma, poor posture, or congenital abnormalities.

The connection between these two conditions lies in the central nervous system. Misalignment in the upper cervical spine can lead to nerve compression and disrupted neural communication. This might contribute to exacerbating fibromyalgia symptoms, particularly neck pain and headaches.

Do we know this for a fact? YES. Surgical treatment for C0-C1 issues in fibromyalgia patients typically involves decompression of the cervical spine. This can be done through procedures like anterior discectomy and instrumented fusion, posterior cervical laminectomy with or without instrumented fusion, or suboccipital decompression. And the success rates are really good.

But here is what they forget:

"These surgeries aim to relieve pressure on the spinal cord and nerves, which can help alleviate pain and improve function. However, it's important to note that surgery is usually considered only after conservative treatments have been tried and if the patient's symptoms are severe."

So why not try chiropractic, PT, acupuncture, etc., to assist the upper cervical region?

Secondly, combining malic acid with magnesium is often considered as a supplementary approach to managing fibromyalgia symptoms:

Malic Acid

Malic acid is a natural substance found in many fruits and vegetables. It plays a significant role in the body's energy production process by participating in the Krebs cycle, which converts nutrients into energy. For individuals with fibromyalgia, malic acid may assist in:

- **Supporting energy production**

- **Reducing muscle pain and tenderness**

- **Improving muscle performance and reducing fatigue**

For more information, you can read about its benefits here.

Magnesium

Studies suggest that a combination of magnesium and malic acid can be more effective in reducing pain and boosting energy levels in fibromyalgia patients compared to either substance alone. This pairing helps address magnesium deficiencies commonly seen in individuals with fibromyalgia.

Metagenics offers a product called **Fibroplex®**, which is designed to support individuals with fibromyalgia and related neuromuscular concerns.

1. Spinal Manipulation: Chiropractic care often involves spinal manipulation, which aims to improve joint mobility and reduce pain levels. Some theories suggest that spinal adjustments might ease the musculoskeletal pain associated with fibromyalgia by improving spinal alignment and reducing muscle tension.

2. Patient Experiences: Many fibromyalgia patients use complementary and alternative medicine, including chiropractic care, to manage their symptoms. Some surveys have indicated high satisfaction rates among patients who have tried chiropractic treatments.

Here's what to look for Radiologically: (This is huge, folks!!)

The first 2 pictures depict the **anterior occiput position**; the skull is basically "sitting" on the first bone in the neck, called the atlas. The next 2 show a widened gap between the skull and atlas; this is **a posterior occiput**, which is much rarer. Adjusted incorrectly, and you never really get better. Often, people get immediately worse; POTs like symptoms can occur despite the incredibly established safety of chiropractic manipulation vs any other conventional therapies.

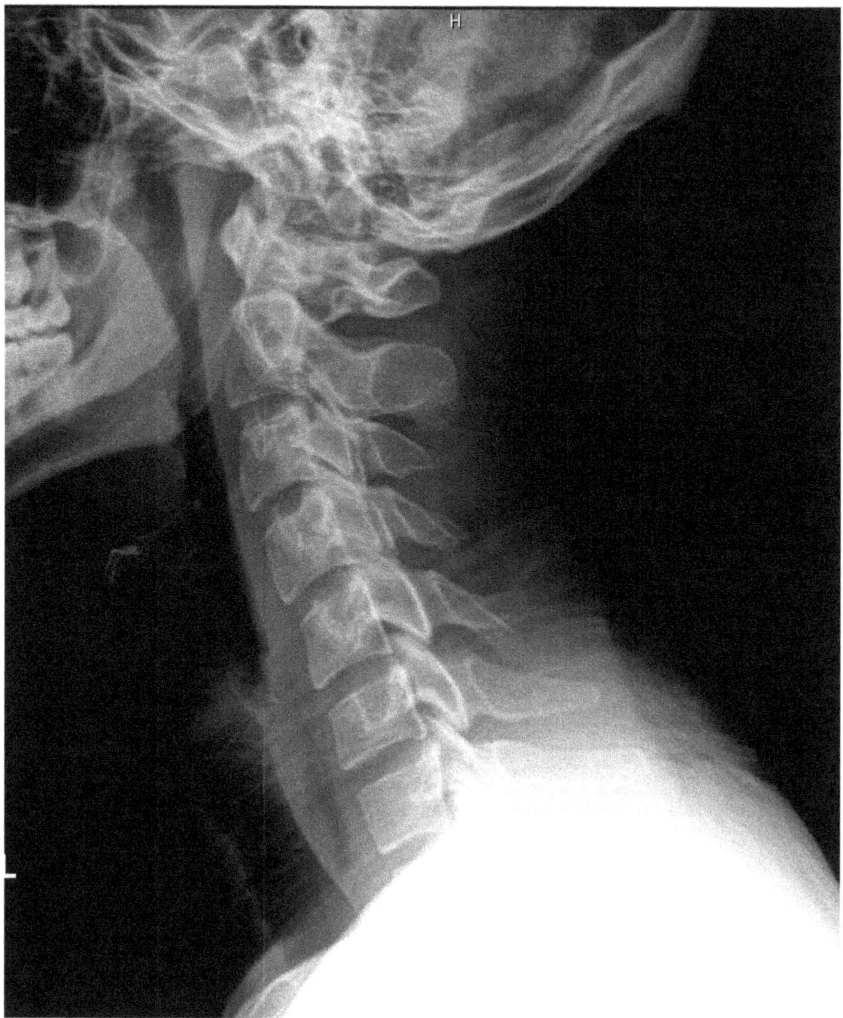

(Anterior Occiput)

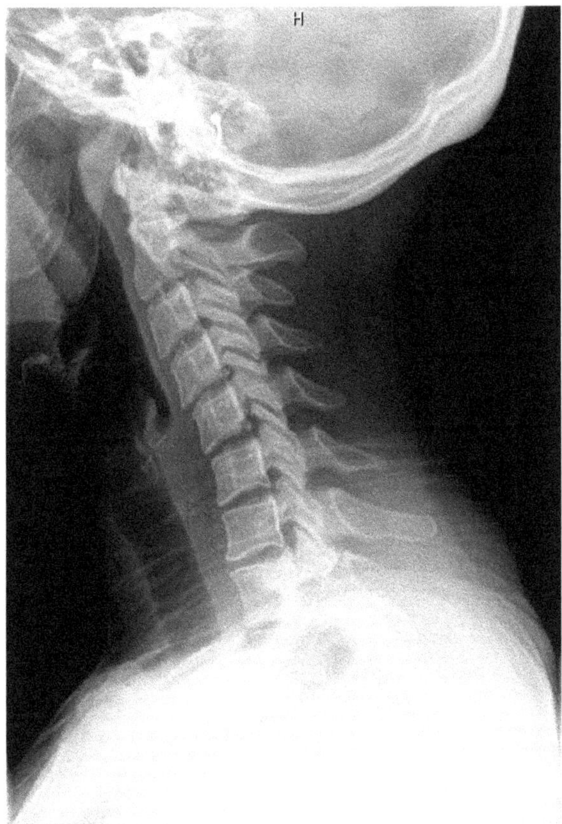

(Anterior occiput)

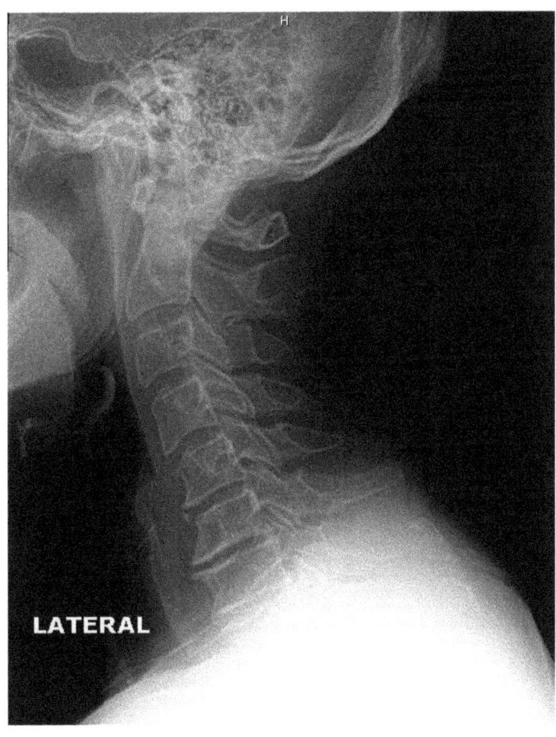

(posterior occiput above)

(Photos courtesy of McAndrews-Jung Chiropractic and Functional Medicine)

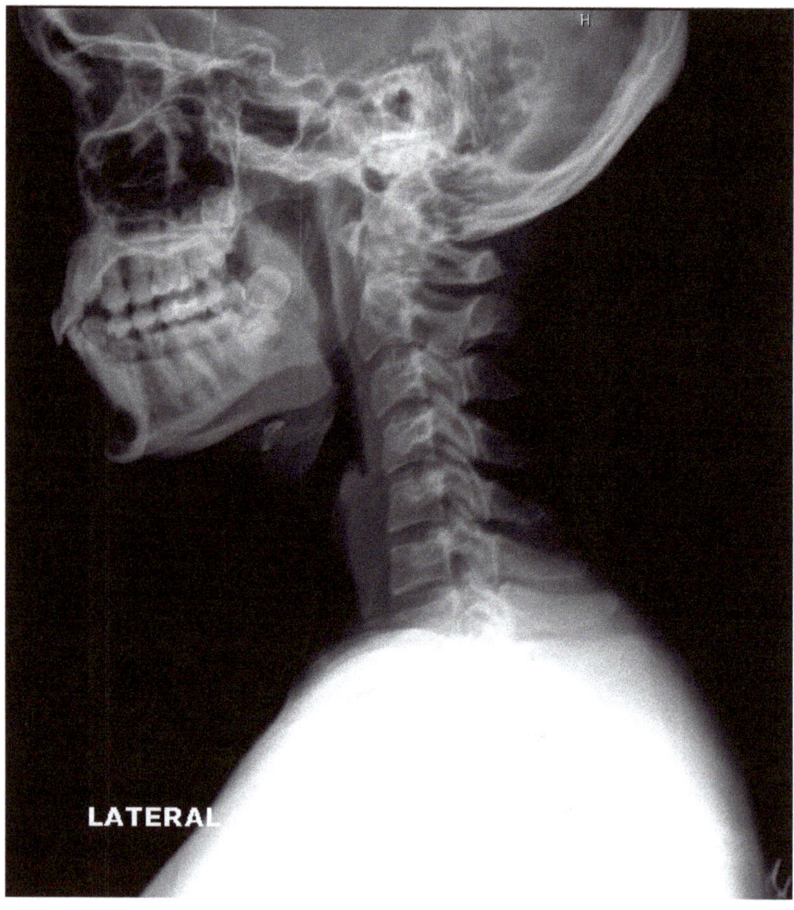

Most radiologists and chiropractors haven't studied anterior vs posterior occiput radiology; it comes with specialized training, so make sure they have experience with it. I have also seen its application in POTS, which most doctors treat as a heart condition, although more frequently, POTS is a problem with the vagus nerve, the longest nerve in the body that pretty much connects everything. (Gut-Brain axis). It runs from the brainstem all the way down to the abdomen, passing numerous organs and playing roles in various bodily functions. It influences things like the heart rate, digestive processes, and even aspects of speech, as well as fibromyalgia.

Head position influences that vagus nerve and even the way you sleep!

The Impact of Sleeping Position on the Vagus Nerve – VagusNerve.com

Herbs & Autoimmunity: Using Botanicals to Balance T-Cell Activity ->>>

Astragalus

Astragalus is an adaptogenic herb that is well known for its use in traditional Chinese medicine to strengthen immune activity. Recent experimental studies on the pharmacological profile of astragalus have shown that the herb can be better described as immune-modulating than immune-stimulating.

The immune-modulating activity of astragalus and its constituents has been well documented in preliminary research studies that suggest that astragalus has great potential in the treatment of autoimmune disease. These results were achieved through the reduction of NF-κB activation, which in turn reduced the secretion of the Th17 inflammatory cytokines TNFα, IL-1ß, IL-6, and IL-17.[11] These results were found to be mediated through ASI-induced reduction of Th1 and Th17 and the promotion of Tregs in the spleen and CNS; changes in cytokines included a reduction of proinflammatory IL-17 and IFNγ and an increase of anti-inflammatory IL-10.

Berberine

Berberine, which is well known for its use in treating digestive and metabolic disruptions, also possesses potent immune-modulating properties. As a result, it has been studied in experimental autoimmune models.

In one study, which examined TNBS-induced Crohn's disease in mice, berberine was found to reduce Th17 and Th1 differentiation, as well as their associated cytokines.[13] In this study, berberine appeared to exert these actions by inhibiting the activation of NF-κB. There have been a number of animal studies on the effects of berberine on IBD, all of which have shown similar patterns of reduced Th1 and Th17 differentiation and the amelioration of IBD symptoms.[14]

Using a Rheumatoid arthritis rat model, berberine was found to improve disease severity, again by reducing cytokines IL-17, IL-6, enhancing IL-10, and TGFß levels – changes that correlated with reduced inflammatory cell infiltration in the synovial joints.

Berberine is often used as a natural alternative to metformin for managing blood sugar levels. While specific dosages can vary, studies and experts commonly recommend **500 mg to 1500 mg per day**, divided into two or three doses. This dosage has been shown to effectively regulate blood sugar and improve insulin sensitivity, similar to metformin.

Curcumin

Curcumin, the active constituent of the rhizome of *Curcuma longa,* is well-known and widely used for its anti-inflammatory, anti-tumor, and immunomodulating properties. Pre-clinical evidence suggests that part of this polyphenol's biological activity can be attributed to its ability to reduce Th17 and restore the balance between Th1/Th2 and Th17/Tregs. Recent in-vivo studies suggest that curcumin's impact on autoimmune disease may involve the reduction and suppression of proinflammatory cytokines (e.g., IL-17, IL-1, IL-6, IL-23, TNFα, and IFNγ), the inhibition of the JAK/STAT and NF-κB intracellular signaling pathways, and the inhibition of Th1 and Th17 differentiation. These mechanisms have been demonstrated in both in-vivo and in-vitro models for myasthenia gravis, systemic lupus erythematosus (SLE), and MS.[3,5,7,20,21]

Milk Thistle

Silybum marianum (milk thistle) is a plant from the Asteraceae family that has been traditionally used for the treatment of liver and gallbladder disorders.

In-vivo and in-vitro studies have revealed silymarin to be a potent anti-inflammatory and immunomodulator, with its main actions including the suppression of NF-κB and its products, the inhibition of TNFα and the downregulation of the Th1 response.[23,24] Another major mechanism by which silymarin works is through the downregulation and inhibition of mTOR, a signaling molecule required for the regulation of adaptive immune cell activation.[25] A recent study by Dupuis et al. found that silibinin upregulated ERß expression, resulting in reduced levels of IL-17 and TNFα in RA patients, possibly through induced apoptosis of Th17 cells.[26]

Skullcap

Scutellaria baicalensis (skullcap) is a popular herb in Chinese medicine. The compound baicalin, a flavonoid isolated from the root of *Scutellaria*, has been found to attenuate the Th17 response in silica-induced lung inflammation and asthma.   In a Rheumatoid mouse study by Yang And in an EAE mouse experiment, baicalin was found to reduce inflammation and demyelination within the CNS. These effects were achieved by attenuating Th1 and Th17 differentiation.

Echinacea is known for its immune-modulating properties, but its effects on the TH17 response are not fully understood. Some studies suggest that echinacea can stimulate immune activity, including the production of cytokines like IL-17, which are associated with TH17 cells. While this stimulation can be beneficial for fighting infections, excessive activation of TH17 cells may contribute to inflammation and autoimmune conditions.

Colostrum, particularly bovine colostrum, has gained attention for its potential benefits in managing autoimmune conditions. It is rich in antibodies, growth factors, and bioactive compounds that may help regulate the immune system and reduce inflammation. Some of its key properties include:

- **Immune Modulation**: Colostrum contains immunoglobulins and cytokines that may help balance immune responses, potentially reducing overactivity in autoimmune conditions.

- **Gut Health**: It supports gut integrity by promoting the growth of beneficial bacteria and repairing the gut lining, which is crucial since a healthy gut can influence immune function.

- **Anti-Inflammatory Effects**: Components like lactoferrin and transforming growth factors (TGF) in colostrum have anti-inflammatory properties that may help manage autoimmune-related inflammation.

TH1 Th2 cytokines again

Sometimes the patient's history will be obvious as to which dominance they have. If Garlic or Echinacea makes you feel worse, there is a good chance you are Th1 dominant autoimmune. If drinking green tea or coffee takes away the pain of your Gout, the possibility exists that you are Th1 dominant; if it makes you feel worse, you may be Th2 dominant. But it is always wise to do the testing!

Other diseases not mentioned here may be helped as follows:

Remember, look up your "disease" and type in to your browser "TH1 or TH2" to know which it is.

Then you can eat accordingly.

Dr. Kharrazian is the practitioner who has developed the protocol for treating autoimmune disease by balancing Th1 and Th2. If Th1 is dominant, he will use Th2 stimulating compounds to raise the level of Th2 and vice versa. In addition, he uses other vitamins and compounds that are known to modulate the balance between Th1 and Th2.

TH1 stimulating compounds:

- Astragalus
- Echinacea

- Medicinal Mushrooms (Maitake and Beta-Glucan are common)
- Glycyrrhiza (found in licorice)
- Melissa Officinalis (Lemon balm)
- Panax Ginseng
- Chlorella
- Grape Seed Extract

TH2 stimulating compounds:

- Caffeine
- Green Tea Extract
- Pine Bark Extract
- White Willow Bark
- Lycopene (found in tomatoes and other red fruits, excluding strawberries and cherries)
- Resveratrol (found in grape skin, sprouted peanuts, and cocoa)
- Pycnogenol (found in the extract of the French maritime pine bark and apples)
- Curcumin (found in turmeric)
- Genistin (found in soybeans)
- Quercitin (a flavonoid found in many fruits and vegetables, such as onions, berries and kale)

Optimal values for fat-soluble vitamins (A, D, E, and K) and minerals (such as magnesium, calcium, zinc, selenium, etc.) are based on a broader understanding of how these nutrients contribute to overall health, often aiming for values that are within optimal ranges rather than the "normal" reference ranges established by conventional medicine. Below are some of the general optimal levels for these vitamins and minerals, but it's important to note that the specific needs can vary depending on individual health conditions, genetics, lifestyle, and environmental factors.

1. Vitamin A (Retinol)

Optimal Range:

- **Serum Retinol**: 50-100 µg/dL (for general health, aiming for balance between deficiency and toxicity)
- **Serum Beta-Carotene (precursor)**: 20-100 µg/dL

Vitamin A is crucial for vision, immune function, and skin health. In functional medicine, both retinol (the active form) and beta-carotene (precursor form) are considered, with an emphasis on dietary sources like liver, egg yolks, and carrots.

2. Vitamin D

Optimal Range (25(OH)D):

- **25-hydroxyvitamin D (25(OH)D)**: 50-80 ng/mL (optimal for immune function, bone health, and inflammation control)

- Some practitioners aim for levels closer to **70-100 ng/mL**, especially for those with autoimmune conditions or chronic inflammation.

Vitamin D is essential for bone health, immune system function, and reducing inflammation. Functional medicine often emphasizes achieving a higher level of vitamin D than the minimum recommended by conventional medicine (20 ng/mL). Sunlight exposure, supplementation, and vitamin D-rich foods (like fatty fish, egg yolks, and fortified foods) are key sources.

3. Vitamin E

Optimal Range:

- **Serum Alpha-Tocopherol:** 12-30 mg/L

- **Vitamin E (as total tocopherol):** 25-50 mg/dL

Vitamin E is a potent antioxidant that helps protect cells from oxidative damage and supports skin, heart, and immune health. Functional medicine often focuses on supplementing with mixed tocopherols and tocotrienols for optimal antioxidant benefits.

4. Vitamin K

Optimal Range:

- **Serum Vitamin K1 (phylloquinone):** 0.1-1.0 ng/mL

- **Serum Vitamin K2 (menaquinone):** No established "optimal" range; however, levels higher than 0.2 ng/mL are considered beneficial for bone and cardiovascular health.

Vitamin K is essential for blood clotting, bone metabolism, and cardiovascular health. Vitamin K2, in particular, is emphasized in functional medicine due to its role in calcium regulation (directing calcium to bones and away from soft tissues like arteries).

5. Magnesium

Optimal Range:

- **Serum Magnesium**: 2.0-2.5 mg/dL (optimal for cellular function, muscle relaxation, and nerve health)

- Some practitioners suggest aiming for levels slightly higher than conventional recommendations, with optimal tissue levels typically found in the **2.2-2.5 mg/dL** range.

Magnesium is involved in over 300 enzymatic processes in the body, including energy production, muscle function, and nervous system regulation. It's common for people to be suboptimal in magnesium, as it's depleted by stress, alcohol consumption, and certain medications.

6. Calcium

Optimal Range:

- **Serum Calcium**: 9.0-10.2 mg/dL
- **Ionized Calcium**: 1.12-1.32 mmol/L

Calcium is necessary for bone health, muscle contraction, and nerve signaling. Functional medicine tends to emphasize the balance between calcium and magnesium, as high calcium intake without adequate magnesium can contribute to muscle cramps, heart arrhythmias, and other issues.

7. Zinc

Optimal Range:

- **Serum Zinc**: 90-120 µg/dL
- **Plasma Zinc**: 80-120 µg/dL

Zinc is critical for immune function, skin health, and wound healing. Many people with autoimmune conditions or chronic illness may be deficient in zinc, so functional medicine often targets levels higher than conventional reference ranges.

8. Selenium

Optimal Range:

- **Serum Selenium**: 110-150 µg/L

Selenium is an important antioxidant and supports thyroid function, immunity, and cardiovascular health. It is commonly used in functional medicine to support those with thyroid conditions like Hashimoto's thyroiditis.

9. Copper

Optimal Range:

- **Serum Copper**: 70-140 µg/dL

Copper is crucial for the formation of red blood cells, immune function, and collagen synthesis. Copper imbalances, whether deficiency or excess, can contribute to health problems, so functional medicine seeks to maintain a balance with other minerals like zinc.

10. Iodine

Optimal Range:

- **Urinary Iodine**: 100-200 µg/L (indicating adequate iodine intake)
- **Serum Iodine**: 60-90 µg/L (varies by individual)

Iodine is essential for thyroid function, and deficiency can lead to goiter and hypothyroidism. Functional medicine supports iodine through dietary sources (e.g., seaweed) and occasionally supplementation when thyroid health requires extra support.

11. Iron

Optimal Range:

- **Serum Ferritin**: 50-150 ng/mL (optimal for most individuals, though this can vary based on sex, age, and health conditions)
- **Serum Iron**: 60-170 µg/dL
- **Transferrin Saturation**: 20-50%

Iron is critical for oxygen transport, energy production, and immune function. Functional medicine often evaluates iron stores (ferritin) as an important marker and addresses both deficiency and excess (as in hemochromatosis). Iron can be problematic in certain autoimmune conditions due to its role in inflammation and oxidative stress. Rheumatoid Arthritis (RA): SLE, IBD and Hemochromatosis. In these cases, **Turmeric** is key for removing excess iron!.

12. Vitamin B12

Optimal Range:

- **Serum B12**: 500-900 pg/mL (optimal range, with some individuals requiring higher levels, especially in cases of methylation disorders)
- **Methylmalonic Acid (MMA)**: Below 250 pmol/L (elevated levels suggest B12 deficiency)

Vitamin B12 is essential for red blood cell production, nerve function, and DNA synthesis. Functional medicine often emphasizes checking B12 status through multiple markers, as deficiency can be subclinical and still cause neurological symptoms. Try sublingual, as older folks don't make intrinsic factors in the gut, necessary to break it down.

13. 5 -Methyl folate, which is the active form of folate (Vitamin B9). It's commonly used for **folate deficiency, mood support, and cardiovascular health**.

- **General Health & Folate Deficiency: 7.5 to 15 mg** per day.
- **Major Depressive Disorder Support: 30 mg** per day.
- **Pregnancy & Prenatal Care: 400 mcg to 1 mg** per day.

Methyl folate is often recommended for individuals with **MTHFR gene mutations**, as they may have difficulty converting folic acid into its active form.

Summary of Functional Medicine Optimal Values:

- **Vitamin A (Retinol):** 50-100 μg/dL
- **Vitamin D:** 50-80 ng/mL (up to 100 ng/mL for certain conditions)
- **Vitamin E:** 12-30 mg/L
- **Vitamin K1/K2:** 0.1-1.0 ng/mL (for K1), >0.2 ng/mL (for K2)
- **Magnesium**: 2.0-2.5 mg/dL
- **Calcium**: 9.0-10.2 mg/dL
- **Zinc**: 90-120 μg/dL
- **Selenium**: 110-150 μg/L
- **Copper**: 70-140 μg/dL
- **Iodine**: Urinary iodine 100-200 μg/L
- **Iron**: Serum ferritin 50-150 ng/mL, Transferrin saturation 20-50%
- **B12**: 500-900 pg/mL

These values reflect the optimal levels often sought in functional medicine to support long-term health.

(For every 1000 D3, NEED 100 K2. Vitamin D3 helps with **calcium absorption**, while Vitamin K2 ensures that calcium is properly directed to the bones and not deposited in arteries. This synergy is crucial for **bone health and cardiovascular function)**

A quick review.

Overall, safe immune boosters for Th1 or Th2 are

Modulators like colostrum and fish oils>>>

EPA (eicosapentaenoic acid) and DHA (docosahexaenoic acid) are omega-3 fatty acids found in fatty cold-water fish like salmon, sardines, and mackerel, as well as in smaller amounts in pastured meats and eggs. These fatty acids play a crucial role in balancing the immune system and reducing inflammation.

Key Benefits of EPA and DHA:

1. Anti-Inflammatory Effects: Both EPA and DHA have anti-inflammatory properties. DHA, in particular, has been shown to have a stronger anti-inflammatory effect compared to EPA.

2. Immune System Balance: EPA and DHA help mediate the immune response, promoting the resolution of inflammation and preventing tissue damage. They support the balance between pro-inflammatory and anti-inflammatory proteins.

3. Neutrophil-to-Lymphocyte Ratio (NLR): Higher levels of EPA and DHA are associated with a lower NLR, indicating a balanced immune system. A balanced NLR is linked to better overall health and reduced risk of chronic diseases.

4. Cognitive and Cardiovascular Health: Omega-3 fatty acids are essential for brain health and cardiovascular function. They have been associated with improved cognitive function, lower risk of dementia, and better cardiovascular health.

5. Heart Disease: The American Heart Association recommends 1,000 mg per day of combined EPA and DHA for people with coronary heart disease or heart failure.

- **High Triglycerides:** For individuals with high triglycerides, a higher dose of 4,000 mg per day is recommended.

- **Depression and Anxiety:** Studies suggest that doses ranging from 200-2,200 mg per day can help reduce symptoms of depression and anxiety.

Safety Considerations

- **Upper Limit:** The European Food Safety Authority suggests that long-term consumption of EPA and DHA supplements at combined doses of up to 5,000 mg per day appears to be safe.

Short-chain fatty acids (SCFAs), particularly butyrate, play a crucial role in maintaining gut health and can be beneficial for conditions like leaky gut syndrome. Here's how SCFAs help:

Benefits of SCFAs for Leaky Gut

1. Gut Barrier Integrity: SCFAs, especially butyrate, serve as the primary energy source for colonocytes (the cells lining the colon). This helps maintain the integrity of the gut barrier, preventing harmful substances from leaking into the bloodstream.

2. Anti-Inflammatory Effects: SCFAs have potent anti-inflammatory properties. Butyrate, in particular, inhibits the activation of pro-inflammatory pathways and promotes the production of anti-inflammatory cytokines.

3. Immune System Regulation: SCFAs support a balanced immune system by influencing the function of regulatory T cells, which help suppress overactive immune responses.

4. Microbiome Health: SCFAs are produced by beneficial gut bacteria through the fermentation of dietary fibers. Maintaining healthy levels of SCFAs supports a diverse and balanced gut microbiome.

How to Increase SCFA Levels

- **Dietary Fiber:** Consuming a diet rich in dietary fibers, such as fruits, vegetables, and legumes, can promote the production of SCFAs by gut bacteria.

- **Prebiotics:** Foods like garlic, onions, bananas, and chicory root contain prebiotics that feed beneficial gut bacteria and increase SCFA production - Metabolic Healing](https://metabolichealing.com/gut-repair-short-chain-fatty-acids-scfas/).

- **Probiotics:** Taking probiotic supplements or consuming probiotic-rich foods like yogurt and kefir can help maintain a healthy gut microbiome and SCFA production.

Metamucil products, including powders and capsules, are gluten-free. They are made from psyllium husk, which does not contain gluten.

Butyrate, a short-chain fatty acid, has been shown to slow the activation of NF-κB, which is a key factor in inflammation. Studies have demonstrated that oral administration of sodium butyrate at doses around 1800 mg per day with meals can help reduce NF-κB activation and inflammation.

Butyrate inhibits NF-kB activation in lamina propria macrophages of patients with ulcerative colitis. Dept. of Medicine, Institute of Pathology, University of Wurzburg, Germany. h.luehrs@medizin.uni-wuerzburg.de

It is the main SCFA (short-chain fatty acid)

Therapeutic Potential of Butyrate

1. Neurological Disorders: Butyrate has shown potential in treating neurological conditions like Alzheimer's disease and Huntington's disease by promoting neuroprotection and reducing inflammation through its epigenetic effects.

2. Inflammatory Diseases: Butyrate's anti-inflammatory properties make it a potential therapeutic agent for inflammatory bowel disease (IBD) and other autoimmune conditions. It helps maintain the integrity of the gut barrier and modulates immune responses.

3. Metabolic Conditions: Butyrate has been studied for its role in improving metabolic health by enhancing insulin sensitivity and reducing obesity-related inflammation.

4. Cancer: As an HDACi, butyrate has demonstrated anti-cancer properties by inducing cancer cell differentiation and apoptosis (programmed cell death). It has been studied in various cancer models for its potential to inhibit tumor growth.

Butter contains small amounts of butyrate (or butyric acid), but it is not pure butyrate. Butyrate is a short-chain fatty acid that is naturally present in dairy products like butter and is produced in the gut when dietary fibers are fermented by gut bacteria.

So, while butter does contain butyrate, consuming it alone wouldn't provide the same concentrated benefits that butyrate supplements might offer.

Certain mushrooms have bioactive compounds that might benefit those with autoimmune disorders. Here are a few notable ones:

1. Chaga (Inonotus obliquus): Known for its anti-inflammatory effects, Chaga mushrooms contain antioxidants and compounds like betulinic acid that could help modulate the immune system.

2. Cordyceps (Ophiocordyceps sinensis): These mushrooms are linked to improved immune regulation, thanks to compounds like polysaccharides and cordycepins.

3. Lion's Mane (Hericium erinaceus): Animal studies suggest Lion's Mane can aid in modulating the immune system and promoting gut health.

4. Maitake (Grifola frondosa): Contains proteoglycan, which has demonstrated immune-boosting and antiviral properties.

There are several herbs, amino acids, and plants that might help balance the immune system and manage autoimmune conditions.

Herbs

- **Turmeric**: Its active compound, curcumin, has potent anti-inflammatory properties and can help regulate the immune system.

- **Ashwagandha:** Known as an adaptogen, it helps balance immune activity by calming it when overactive and stimulating it when underactive. When it comes to ashwagandha, it's important to stick to recommended dosages to minimize the risk of side effects and ensure you get the most benefit. Here are some general guidelines:

General Dosage Recommendations:

- **Standardized Root Extract:** Typically, 300 to 500 mg per day of a standardized extract containing 5% withanolides.

- **Raw Powder:** If you're using raw ashwagandha powder, doses can range from 1 to 6 grams per day, divided into 2-3 doses.

- **Tinctures and Liquid Extracts:** Follow the manufacturer's instructions, but a common recommendation is around 1-2 mL, 1-3 times daily.

- **For Stress and Anxiety:** A common dose is 600 mg per day, usually divided into two doses of 300 mg each.

- **For Sleep:** Taking 300-500 mg before bedtime can help with sleep quality.

- **For Overall Well-being:** Following the typical 300-500 mg per day dosage works well for general health benefits.

Ginger: Offers strong anti-inflammatory effects and can soothe the gut, which is important for immune regulation. Ginger root has long been recognized for its anti-inflammatory potential, making it an attractive natural treatment for autoimmune conditions. Here's a summary based on recent findings:

Dosage:

- **Typical Supplementation:** A common dosage is around 1,000 to 2,000 mg per day of ginger root extract. For specific conditions, doses such as 20 mg of gingerols per day (a component of ginger) have also been studied.

- **Ginger Tea:** Consuming ginger tea made from about 2 to 4 grams of fresh ginger daily can also help.

- **Capsules and Tablets:** Follow the instructions on the supplement packaging, usually involving 500-1,000 mg capsules taken 1-2 times daily.

Side Effects:

- **Common:** Heartburn, diarrhea, stomach discomfort, and mouth irritation.

- **Serious:** Excessive bleeding (especially in people with bleeding disorders or those on blood thinners) and potential interactions with medications for diabetes or high blood pressure.

Licorice Root: Has adaptogenic and anti-inflammatory properties that support a healthy immune response. You can overdose on licorice root. The primary compound in licorice root, glycyrrhizin, can cause serious health issues if consumed in large amounts. Overconsumption can lead to a condition called pseudohyperaldosteronism, which mimics the effects of elevated aldosterone and can result in high blood pressure, low potassium levels, and disturbances in your body's acid-base balance.

1. Traditional Use: Many herbalists suggest no more than 2-4 grams of dried licorice root per day, typically in the form of tea or tincture.

2. Hydrolyzed Extract (DGL): Deglycyrrhizinated licorice (DGL) is considered safer, especially for long-term use, since it has had most of the glycyrrhizin removed. The recommended dosage for DGL can vary but generally ranges from 380-1140 mg per day.

This is a must-have for GUT REPAIR formulas.

Andrographis paniculata, often dubbed the "King of Bitters," is a remarkable herb renowned for its potent immunomodulatory properties.

Andrographis acts as an immune balancer, adept at fine-tuning the body's defense mechanisms. It doesn't merely stimulate or suppress the immune response; instead, it modulates it, ensuring optimal functionality.

Andrographis tends to favor a shift toward the Th1 response, enhancing the body's ability to combat viral and certain bacterial infections. It stimulates the production of key cytokines like interferon-gamma (IFN-γ) and interleukin-2 (IL-2), which are crucial for Th1 activity.

However, what's fascinating is that Andrographis doesn't push the immune system into overdrive. It helps maintain a balance between Th1 and Th2 responses.

The magic of Andrographis lies in its active compounds, particularly andrographolide:

- **Anti-Inflammatory Effects:** Andrographolide has been shown to reduce pro-inflammatory cytokines like TNF-α and IL-6, curbing excessive inflammation.

- **Antioxidant Properties:** It combats oxidative stress by neutralizing free radicals, which can otherwise damage cells and disrupt immune function.

- **Antimicrobial Activity:** Andrographis exhibits direct antimicrobial effects against certain pathogens, providing a multi-faceted defense.

- **Enhancing Immune Response:** Studies indicate that Andrographis can boost the immune system's ability to fight off infection, particularly upper respiratory tract infections.

- **Autoimmune Conditions:** In cases where the immune system is overactive, Andrographis may help modulate the response, potentially offering relief in conditions like rheumatoid arthritis.

- **Synergistic Effects:** When combined with other herbs like echinacea, andrographis's immune-enhancing effects can be amplified.

- **Standard Dosage:** Typically, 400 to 600 mg of standardized Andrographis extract, containing andrographolide 4-6%, taken two to three times daily.

- **Duration:** For acute conditions, it's often used for short-term periods of up to 10 days. For immune support, consult a healthcare professional for guidance on longer use.

Potential Side Effects and Precautions

- **Digestive Upset:** Some may experience stomach discomfort, diarrhea, or loss of appetite.

- **Allergic Reactions:** Rare but possible, especially in individuals allergic to plants in the Acanthaceae family.

- **Pregnancy and Breastfeeding:** Not recommended due to insufficient safety data.

- **Medication Interactions:** Andrographis may interact with immunosuppressive drugs or anticoagulants. Always consult a healthcare provider if you're on medication.

Amino Acids

- **Glutamine:** Supports gut health and immune function and can help repair the intestinal lining.

- **Lysine:** Plays a role in reducing inflammation and promoting immune balance.

- **Threonine:** Important for the production of antibodies and helps maintain a healthy immune system. Threonine is an essential amino acid that plays a critical role in maintaining the immune system. One of its key functions is to modulate the immune response by influencing the production of cytokines—these are signaling molecules that help regulate immune reactions. Here's how threonine impacts the immune system:

- **Threonine and Cytokine Production:** Threonine is involved in the synthesis of proteins, including immune proteins and cytokines. The amino acid supports both the innate and adaptive immune responses by promoting the production of interleukins and other cytokines.

- **Threonine and Gut Health:** This amino acid is crucial for the maintenance and function of the gastrointestinal tract, where a significant portion of the immune system resides. By supporting gut health and mucin production, threonine indirectly affects cytokine levels and immune system responses.

- **Threonine and T-helper Cells:** Threonine aids in the functioning of T-helper cells, which play a key role in orchestrating the immune response by secreting cytokines.

Plants

- **Aloe Vera:** Known for its soothing and anti-inflammatory effects, it can help support immune function.

- **Green Tea:** Contains antioxidants and polyphenols that can modulate the immune system and reduce inflammation.

Magnesium plays a pivotal role in your immune system's function.

How Magnesium Influences the Immune System:

1. Activation of Immune Cells: Magnesium is essential for the activation and proliferation of lymphocytes, which are white blood cells that fight off invaders like viruses and bacteria. Without adequate magnesium, these cells can't function optimally.

2. Regulation of Inflammation: It helps modulate inflammatory responses by affecting cytokine production—those are the signaling proteins that tell immune cells where to go and what to do. Magnesium ensures that inflammation is appropriate and doesn't spiral out of control.

3. Oxidative Stress Reduction: Magnesium acts as a co-factor for antioxidant enzymes, helping neutralize free radicals that can damage cells, including immune cells. This means it protects the immune system from the wear and tear of daily life.

4. Stress Response and Immunity: Chronic stress can weaken the immune system, and magnesium plays a role in regulating the body's stress response by influencing cortisol levels. Adequate magnesium can help keep stress in check, indirectly supporting immune health.

Incorporating magnesium-rich foods into your diet is a natural way to support your immune system:

- **Leafy Greens:** Spinach, kale, and Swiss chard are excellent sources.

- **Nuts and Seeds:** Almonds, cashews, pumpkin seeds, and sunflower seeds pack a magnesium punch.

- **Fish:** Fatty fish like mackerel and salmon contain magnesium and omega-3 fatty acids, which are also beneficial for immune health.

- **Dark Chocolate:** A delightful treat that offers magnesium—just opt for varieties with at least 70% cocoa.

Dosage Guidelines: The Recommended Dietary Allowance (RDA) for adults ranges from 310 to 420 mg per day, depending on age and sex.

- **- Types of Supplements:**

    o **Magnesium Citrate and Glycinate:** Known for better absorption and gentler effects on the digestive system.

    o **Magnesium Oxide:** Contains a higher amount of elemental magnesium but is less bioavailable.

Magnesium bisglycinate, also known as magnesium glycinate, is a highly bioavailable form of magnesium that is gentle on the digestive system. It's often used to support heart health, including conditions like mitral valve prolapse (MVP).

Magnesium bisglycinate helps to regulate blood pressure and maintain a steady heart rhythm, which can be particularly beneficial for individuals with mitral valve prolapse. It also supports overall cardiovascular health by promoting vascular relaxation and reducing inflammation. Do you know someone with panic attacks? This is my "Golden fix" for that.

Beyond the immune system, magnesium is involved in over 300 biochemical reactions in the body, including:

- **Energy Production:** It's crucial for ATP synthesis, the energy currency of your cells.

- **Muscle and Nerve Function:** Magnesium helps regulate muscle contractions and nerve signals.

- **Bone Health:** It works alongside calcium and vitamin D to maintain strong bones.

- **Heart Rhythm:** Essential for maintaining a steady and normal heartbeat.

Extra Information:

BIOFILM CLR for your Guts

Biofilm-clearing ingredients are compounds that help disrupt and break down biofilms, which are protective layers formed by bacteria and fungi. Here are some commonly studied ingredients:

1. Enzymes:

- **Serrapeptase:** Breaks down proteins in biofilms.

- **Nattokinase:** Helps dissolve fibrin, a component of biofilms.

- **Proteolytic Enzymes:** Aid in degrading the biofilm matrix.

2. Natural Extracts:

- **Garlic Extract (Allicin):** Known for its antimicrobial and biofilm-disrupting properties.

- **Grapefruit Seed Extract:** Effective against bacterial biofilms.

- **Berberine:** Has biofilm-clearing and antimicrobial effects.

3. Chelating Agents:

- **EDTA (Ethylenediaminetetraacetic Acid):** Binds to metals that stabilize biofilms, weakening their structure.

4. Essential Oils:

- **Tea Tree Oil:** Disrupts biofilms and has antimicrobial properties.

- **Oregano Oil:** Contains carvacrol, which is effective against biofilms.

5. Other Compounds:

- **Xylitol:** Prevents biofilm formation, especially in the oral cavity.

- **Colloidal Silver:** Known for its antimicrobial effects and biofilm disruption.

6. Homocysteine and Parkinson's Disease:

- Müller, T., & Werne, B. (2004). "Homocysteine levels in patients with Parkinson's disease treated with levodopa/entacapone combination." Neurology, 62(2), 390-391.

Interesting Facts:

If you are taking a GLP injection, please know that:

It has been shown to keep muscle mass after age 55, you'll need leucine 2.5 g each meal. Am. J Clin. Nutr. February 2025Volume 121Issue 2

- While studies show people on GLP1 lose 40% of muscle, this is critical. When you are older, it's called sarcopenia (muscle wasting). While the "experts" claim Leucine did not increase muscle mass in the older population, they forgot to admit that in studies on supplementation, leucine is known to increase muscle protein synthesis, which can help in preventing muscle wasting.

- For best results, combining leucine supplementation with resistance training has been shown to be more effective in improving muscle mass and strength.

- **Aging and balance:** Take 7.5 g leucine to avoid sarcopenia, not an RDA of 2.9.

- Leucine plays a crucial role in **muscle protein synthesis**, and research suggests that higher doses may be beneficial for preventing **sarcopenia (age-related muscle loss)**. 7.5 g may be more effective in stimulating muscle growth and preventing muscle deterioration in older adults.

- Leucine is often combined with **resistance training** and other **branched-chain amino acids (BCAAs)** to maximize its effects. The best is chicken thighs and legs, and beef skirt steakas natural source. Since sarcopenia leads to **muscle weakness and loss of strength**, it can make it harder to maintain stability, increasing the risk of **falls and fractures**. The condition impacts **walking ability, coordination, and overall mobility**, making daily activities more challenging.

- "Perspective: Developing a Nutrient-Based Framework for Protein Quality" by Shavawn M. Forester, Emily M. Jennings-Dobbs, Shazia A. Sathar, and Donald K. Layman, Journal of Nutrition August 2023

- **Weak heart:** Hawthorn root is known for its cardiotonic properties, which means it can help strengthen the heart muscle and improve its function. It is often used to treat heart conditions like heart failure and high blood pressure.

- Drugs for a weak heart :

- Coreg is often prescribed alongside other medications like diuretics and ACE inhibitors to improve survival rates and reduce hospitalizations due to heart failure for Heart Disease | It's important to take Coreg exactly as prescribed by your healthcare provider and not to stop taking it abruptly, as this can worsen your condition for Heart Disease |

Supplement with:

1. Garlic: Garlic is well-known for its heart-healthy benefits, including improving blood circulation and reducing cholesterol levels.

2. Arjuna Bark: This herb has been used traditionally to strengthen the heart muscle and improve blood flow.

3. Bilberry: Bilberry is known for its ability to strengthen vascular walls and improve microcirculatory health.

4. Green Tea: Rich in antioxidants, green tea can improve the health of blood vessels and the heart.

5. CoQ10 For heart health, including conditions like heart failure, the typical recommended dosage ranges from **100 to 300 mg per day**, divided into two doses. Some studies suggest that higher doses, up to **600 mg per day**, may be beneficial for individuals with severe heart conditions, but this should always be done under medical supervision.

6. Hawthorn root: Studies often recommend **160-1800 mg of standardized hawthorn extract daily**, divided into two or three doses.

Here are some key medical references related to the topics we discussed:

1. Testosterone and Autoimmune Diseases:

- Cutolo, M., & Straub, R. H. (2009). "Sex hormones and immune response in rheumatoid arthritis." Clinical and Experimental Rheumatology, 27(2 Suppl 53), S18-S20.

- Whitacre, C. C., Reingold, S. C., & O'Looney, P. A. (1999). "A gender gap in autoimmunity." Science, 283(5406), 1277-1278.

2. DHEA and Autoimmune Diseases:

- Casson, P. R., Andersen, R. N., Herrod, H. G., & Carson, S. A. (1993). "Oral dehydroepiandrosterone in physiologic doses modulates immune function in postmenopausal women." American Journal of Obstetrics and Gynecology, 169(6), 1536-1539.

- Straub, R. H., & Cutolo, M. (2001). "Involvement of the hypothalamic-pituitary-adrenal/gonadal axis and the peripheral nervous system in rheumatoid arthritis: Viewpoint based on a systemic pathogenetic role." Arthritis & Rheumatism, 44(3), 493-507.

- O'Suilleabhain, P., & Dewey, R. B. (2002). "Homocysteine and levodopa toxicity in PD." Neurology, 59(10), 1583-1584.

3. Glyphosate and Cytochrome P450:

- Samsel, A., & Seneff, S. (2013). "Glyphosate, pathways to modern diseases II: Celiac sprue and gluten intolerance." Interdisciplinary Toxicology, 6(4), 159-184.

- Mesnage, R., Bernay, B., & Séralini, G. E. (2012). "Ethoxylated adjuvants of glyphosate-based herbicides are active principles of human cell toxicity." Toxicology, 313(2-3), 122-128.

(++)Some articles from medical journals that discuss the connection between brain injuries and gut issues:

1. Dysregulated brain-gut axis in the setting of traumatic brain injury: review of mechanisms and anti-inflammatory pharmacotherapies. This review article from the Journal of Neuroinflammation explores the mechanisms of brain-gut axis dysfunction post-TBI and discusses various anti-inflammatory pharmacotherapies that could help mitigate inflammation along the brain-gut axis. Dysregulated brain-gut axis in the setting of traumatic brain injury: review of mechanisms and anti-inflammatory pharmacotherapies | Journal of Neuroinflammation | Full Text

2. Bowel dysfunctions after acquired brain injury: a scoping review. Published in Frontiers in Human Neuroscience, this scoping review examines the extent and type of evidence on bowel dysfunction after acquired brain injury (ABI) and presents conservative treatment options. Frontiers | Bowel dysfunctions after acquired brain injury: a scoping review

3. The Role of Macronutrients and Gut Microbiota in Neuroinflammation Post-Traumatic Brain Injury: A Narrative Review. This narrative review from the journal Nutrients discusses the relationship between dietary macronutrients, gut microbiota, and neuroinflammation in TBI, suggesting that targeted nutrition and gut health optimization could serve as promising therapeutic modalities. The Role of Macronutrients and Gut Microbiota in Neuroinflammation Post-Traumatic Brain Injury: A Narrative Review

Dr . Jung can be reached at Thrivein45@gmail to secure your free 15-minute consultation.

I wish you the best on your health journey!

Dr. John W Jung MS DC FIAMA FACMUAP